REGRET AT ROOSEVELT RANCH

ROOSEVELT RANCH BOOK FOUR

ELISE FABER

Elise Faber
SNARKY BOOKS FOR SNARKY MINDS

ROOSEVELT RANCH SERIES

Disaster at Roosevelt Ranch

Heartbreak at Roosevelt Ranch

Collision at Roosevelt Ranch

Regret at Roosevelt Ranch

Desire at Roosevelt Ranch

Owen,
You're awesome, kind, and beyond wonderful.
Never stop being you.
I love you.

PROLOGUE

Henry

HENRY WIPED down the final table. He was beyond ready to go home and crash after a busy Sunday evening cooking at the diner.

He'd already flicked off the neon "Open" sign and dimmed the lights. The kitchen had been scrubbed and reset for the next morning's breakfast rush, and he'd sent Tilly off about an hour earlier—she'd had a date, and Henry didn't mind sweeping up or stocking the tables with all the necessities for the next day.

Paper napkins, ketchup, salt and pepper, sugar. They weren't what had been on the tables in the Michelin-starred restaurant he'd cooked at while living in New York five years before, but they were his childhood.

His way of feeling close to his dad.

God, he missed his dad.

The bell hanging on the front door rang, and he mentally cursed at having forgotten to lock it.

Beginner mistake.

He'd worked half his childhood in the diner, had closed it down more times than he could count.

And somehow, he'd forgotten to lock the front door.

Hopeless.

"I'm sorry, we're closed," he said, deliberately not looking as he reached to straighten a salt shaker that was slightly askew.

"So, this is your place, is it?" The softly accented voice made him freeze.

Italy. Warm Tuscan sunlight, softly rolling hills through wine country. Cheese and pasta and pizza and . . . *her.*

He accidentally knocked the shaker to the floor. It didn't break because this was a family place and they'd learned long ago that plastic was safer with the kiddos, but Henry watched in slow horror as the lid popped off and salt spread out on the tile floor.

Though his horror didn't come from the spilled salt.

No. It came from the fact that she was there.

He turned. Saw for sure he hadn't been mistaken.

She was there.

Isabella Mariano was in Darlington, Utah. Inside his restaurant.

"*Buona notte*, Henry."

He'd last seen her as she'd gotten on a plane heading the opposite direction of where he'd needed her, flying away when he'd asked her to stay, bolting while his heart had been left to shatter.

"Isabella," he said coldly.

If she noticed his tone, she didn't comment on it.

Then again, she was good at that.

"What are you doing here?" he prompted when she didn't say anything further.

She swept over to him, heels clicking on the tile floor, more beautiful than ever. Her brown hair fell in perfect waves, her killer body was clad in sleek designer clothes, and a diamond ring on her left ring finger sparkled in the dim light.

Diamond ring.

On her left hand.

He processed that, but her words still hit him like a two-by-four to the temple.

"I want you to cater my wedding."

ONE

Henry

HENRY WAS MAKING A MOTHERFUCKING Cobb salad.

Fuck it.

He was already in Hell. He might as well embrace it.

He slammed the metal bowl onto the counter, grabbed a head of romaine lettuce from the walk-in—and only romaine, because fuck the tasteless, useless iceberg variety—then walked back over to the stainless steel table that had served as the prep area for the last three decades Henry's had been open.

His dad's favorite meal.

The first quaintly American—Isabella's wording, not his, because Henry would have called it old-fashioned and boring—thing that he'd cooked for the woman who he'd once hoped to marry.

The woman who'd abandoned him before he could ask, who'd left him when he'd had to go home and take care of his dying father.

The woman who'd supposedly loved him.

His eggs had five more minutes on the stove—because if he

was replicating his dad's favorite recipe, Henry figured he might as well also use the tricks his father had taught him as well. Thus, he'd boiled the eggs for three minutes then turned off the heat and covered them for another eighteen. He'd get perfectly yellow yokes without any unseemly green outer layer.

Worked. Every time.

"Fuck," he muttered.

The only difference between his version and his dad's was the quality of the produce. Fresh tomatoes from his garden, organic eggs and chicken from a local farmer, ridiculously expensive but delicious bacon.

Sighing, he washed the lettuce and shredded the chicken breast then chopped and fried up the bacon so it was in mouth-wateringly, some might say *heavenly*, crispy bites. After setting it aside to drain, he spun and grabbed the eggs from the burner, peeling them with a practiced efficiency that only came from working close to twenty years in this very kitchen.

The white tore, exposing the perfect yellow yoke inside.

Rookie move.

"Dammit." Henry dropped his chin to his chest and sighed. He wanted to throw the egg in the trash, but he had too much damned respect for the food that came into his kitchen to do such a thing. Instead, he set it aside to turn into egg salad later. Then he peeled the next egg.

No torn white on this one.

He grabbed his favorite knife and a heartbeat later perfectly even portions of egg lay on his cutting board. Next came the avocado.

"What are you doing?"

The voice made him jump and his knife slipped, slicing through his fingertip as easily as it had the egg earlier. He held back his f-bomb only because the voice that had startled him hadn't belonged to an adult.

He gritted his teeth, wrapped his hand in a towel, and turned to face Allie.

Her mom, and his long-time friend Melissa, stood behind her daughter, eyes trailing from his hand to the ingredients on his board.

Kelly would have been better.

Melissa's sister and his best friend was hopeless when it came to food. *She* wouldn't be able to tell the difference between some lettuce and fixings in a bowl and the component parts of a Cobb salad.

Melissa, on the other hand?

She was a celebrity chef, complete with her own cooking show and cookbooks and an absolutely huge social media following. She definitely knew the ingredients of a Cobb salad.

"Who ordered the Cobb?" she asked, walking over to the metal strip that held any outstanding tickets. "The town knows that you don't like making it. Someone have it in for you?"

He snorted.

Someone had it in for him, all right.

Her gaze trailed over the open tickets, no doubt seeing that no one had actually ordered the salad. He opened his mouth to come up with an excuse for why he was making it—aside from punishing himself that was.

Melissa raised her brows.

Henry just shrugged.

What *could* he say?

Bella had swept back into his life and driven him insane again?

Accurate, but more information than he was willing to share.

Luckily, Melissa didn't know *why* the thought of making this particular dish always struck a chord with him.

She didn't understand that it was the combination of past

and present, of Isabella and his father, of pain and heartbreak and a really, *really* dark time. She also didn't know that he had finally been moving on with his life, finally dating again and thinking about the future when who had waltzed into the restaurant less than twelve hours before?

The source of that pain and heartbreak and really dark time.

Or, *one* of the sources anyway. Because he couldn't put his father's death all on Isabella. She didn't cause his dad's heart attack or the triple bypass surgery or the subsequent complications after the surgery.

But she hadn't been there.

Henry had asked, and Isabella hadn't come.

And now she wanted him to cater her fucking wedding?

Yeah, that would happen as soon as Hell got its first snowy day.

Allie grabbed his wrist and gently peeled back the towel. Normally, Henry would have reacted faster, stopped her from seeing. But Isabella had rotted his brain, and he definitely was *not* operating on all cylinders. Allie's eyes filled with tears. "Uncle Henry, I'm sorry. I—"

He finally got his shit together.

Squatting down in front of her, he brought his hand behind his back. "Not your fault," he said and wiped away one of the glistening drops that slid free from her eyes to drip down her cheeks. "All this for a little scratch?"

"Th-that's more than a scratch—"

It was.

But he wasn't going to tell a first-grader that.

"Nope," he said. "I've had way worse. This is nothing. Your mommy will slap a Band-Aid on for me, and I'll be good as new."

"Band-Aids make everything better." She nodded sagely.

He chucked her under her chin and walked over to the kit

that he kept on hand for just this reason. Not that he usually needed to use it. Typically, it was his part-time chef who'd been wounded. Not Henry.

Cuts. Catering weddings. So many new things.

Lucky him.

Stifling a sigh, Henry pulled out the kit then began washing the cut. "What are we learning how to cook today?"

He and Allie had been having weekly cooking lessons every Monday afternoon after she got out of school. It had started when Melissa had needed a spare set of adult eyes to keep track of Allie while she'd been filming and all other available adults had been busy working.

Desperate, she'd called him, and Henry . . . well, the kitchen had seen plenty of kiddos over the years. It wasn't a big deal. He'd pulled out his old metal stool, positioned it next to him at the counter, and put Allie to work tearing basil leaves.

He'd taught Allie what a Caprese salad was that day.

She'd surprised him by being all-in to make homemade mozzarella cheese.

And he'd started living again.

So, Allie came by on Mondays.

Henry *knew* that. Which meant he shouldn't have been surprised by her appearance, shouldn't have allowed himself to be so caught up in the tangled fucking bullshit from his past that he hadn't heard her coming.

First-graders *weren't* quiet.

Case in point, Allie, tears now forgotten, pounding over to the hook that held her hot pink apron, yanking it off, and tying it on before walking quickly—because one of the first rules he'd had to be strict with her about was absolutely no running in the kitchen—over to where her stool stood along one wall and dragging it in place.

He and Melissa winced at a particularly loud screech.

"You don't have to keep doing this, you know," Melissa murmured, grabbing his hand from beneath the water and putting her Mom Skills to work.

"I like doing *this*," he said. "Plus, give that babysitter of yours a break every once in a while."

"You mean me? Or Rob? Because you certainly can't mean Kelly." Her lips twitched. "She's got her hands more than full with the twins and Abby."

Henry nudged her shoulder. "Why do you seem gleeful about that?"

"Only because she gave me the biggest runaround in middle and high school."

"Good of you to admit it." He flexed his fingers when Melissa finished with the bandage, testing his grip, and then slipped on a rubber glove so he could finish his shift and still be sanitary.

"I want to make a Brad Recipe!" Allie said, or rather yelled.

Because first-graders—or at least *this* one—were not quiet.

And though Henry wished he could say his flinch was volume-related, it wasn't.

Because Brad was *his* dad. And a Brad Recipe was one that came straight from his father's box of handwritten index cards. Allie had stumbled onto them a few months back, and it had been fine. The five years that had passed since he'd lost his dad hadn't made the pain go away, but they did make the memories more palatable.

Henry could actually remember the good things.

Not succumb to regret and that huge yawning cavern that was in the place where his dad should be.

He swallowed hard, but forced out an "Okay."

Which was all the encouragement Allie needed. She sprinted over to the shelf and pulled down the little plastic box then proceeded to search through it with all the relish of a girl after his own heart.

Food. Learning new techniques and recipes.

He dug chicks who were into food.

Like Isabella.

Fuck, he'd fallen for her hook, line, and sinker.

Melissa touched his shoulder. "You sure you're"—her eyes trailed to the ingredient-laden board from his ill-advised Cobb salad—"up for this today?"

"Go." He pushed her in the direction of the door. "Do fancy TV things. I've got this."

She paused, turned back. "It's just dubs, and I'll reimburse you for the ingred—"

"Shh." Another nudge since this was the same argument they had week after week. He didn't need to be reimbursed for hanging with Allie. He loved the kid, just as much as he loved Kelly and Melissa and all their respective kiddos. They were family, and you didn't charge family. Nope. No way. No how. "Go on now with you. Enjoy being a big-time chef."

Her lips twitched, but she nodded and left, pressing a kiss to the top of Allie's head as she did so.

Henry crossed over to his partner in crime. "So, what are we making?"

"This one!"

He glanced at the card she held up. "Black Forest Icebox Cake," he read. "One of my favorites." He dropped his voice to a whisper. "We can also swap out the cherries and dark chocolate and make a cookies and cream version."

Her eyes went wide. "Really?"

"Really really."

She jumped up from the stool. "I'll grab the cookies!"

"No samples on the way," he called.

Allie's shoulders dropped slightly in disappointment—

Henry knew all her tricks by now—but she didn't stop moving until she'd returned with the cookies and the rest of the ingredients he called out to her.

Once everything was set out and measured, she pushed up her sleeves and clapped her hands once. "Let's get to work."

Henry grinned as he handed her the cream to whip up in the mixer.

"Yes, let's."

Work was exactly what he should be focusing on.

TWO

Isabella

SUNLIGHT STREAMED through the window of Darlington's only bed and breakfast, hitting her straight in her jet-lagged, emotionally exhausted brain.

Wincing, she rolled over and jammed a pillow over her head, desperate for a few more hours of sleep. She'd gone to bed too early then had been up most of the night before falling back asleep just as the first rays of sunshine had begun peeking over the hills in the distance.

The sun was well into the sky now, illuminating the tiny town that Henry called home.

In some ways, it reminded her of *her* small town, barely a blip on the surrounding geography, only a few streets to its name, and only a couple of thousand residents.

But where her home had been cold, this place was warm.

And she didn't mean temperature either.

There was life to Darlington, warmth and softness, and . . . she was letting herself get lost in fantasy. She'd grown up in

Italy for God's sake. That was the definition of warm, especially in the summer months.

Maybe it was the people.

Or rather, the absence of *some* people.

Shaking her head at herself, she braved the bright light and sat up. Isabella reached for her cell on the nightstand and groaned. Thankfully, she'd set it to *do not disturb*, because otherwise the sheer multitude of calls, texts, and voicemails would have turned her minimal sleep into no sleep.

"Fuck," she muttered and dropped it to the bed.

It had been stupid to run, she knew that. But it had been even stupider to come back here and think that she could repair what she'd shattered before.

Especially when she led with, *"I want you to cater my wedding."*

She wasn't getting married.

Or, not any longer anyway.

That she'd thought she could go through with the whole thing had been a . . . mistake.

Huge understatement.

Snorting, she slid from the bed and walked into the bathroom then twisted the taps inside the shower until hot water poured out and began filling the room with steam.

Her father was a persuasive man and the thought of being persuaded down that particular avenue—read: lifelong commitment and *marriage*—had finally snapped her back to reality.

He had already prompted her to make the biggest mistake of her life.

She didn't need him coaxing or cajoling, or whatever synonym that wasn't popping into her head at the moment, her into Huge Life Mistake Version Two. Isabella had been weak for the past five years. That was long enough. It was time she got her head out of her ass, act like the grown woman she was, and live her fucking life.

And she wanted to live that life with Henry.

Which she'd pretty much screwed up since her first words to him were about catering a wedding she'd run away from.

But, dammit, it was the first thing that had popped into her head when she'd seen him there, looking as gorgeous as ever. Her throat had tightened, her pulse spiked, and she'd felt like she was going to faint. All she could think was *this is right*.

Henry was right.

She'd been meeting with wedding planners and florists and cake decorators and caterers and—

She'd. Just. Blurted.

The first thing to come to her mind.

Which had pretty much been the worst thing. Henry had been on the defensive, closed down and eyes cold before she'd verbal diarrhead that nonsense. After? Well, his expression had been telling those ice caps in the Himalayas they were too warm.

So she'd fled.

Whirling around and hightailing out of the diner and back across the street to the bed and breakfast. Once safely ensconced in her room, she realized she was starving, but everything in town was closed and no room service was to be found. Isabella had not so successfully filled her empty stomach with stale crackers and tap water.

Such a gourmet meal for a professional chef.

Not that she'd been doing much "chefing" as of late. That had been a moment of rebellion, according to her father.

Heaven forbid she find something she was passionate about and dive in.

Heaven forbid . . . she have a fucking spine.

Isabella sighed as she stripped and stepped into the shower, letting the hot water flow down her head, her hair, her nape. She rested her head against the tile wall and tried to center herself, to find the cool and calm woman she'd been since she'd walked away from Henry.

But that woman was in hiding, camouflaged like a son of a bitch, and currently unreachable.

Henry was mad. Hurt. Cold.

Of course he was.

Because he didn't know.

And instead of telling him, she'd waltzed in and tried to hire him. Which was *so* something her father would do. Throw money at a problem until it resolved itself one way or another.

"Ugh." She sighed again, letting the water stream over her until her stomach rumbled, protesting her last meal of crackers and the long stretch of airline and airport food before that. Her flight had been via first class, but try as they might, plane food was still just that . . . and *that* wasn't great.

She needed fuel and to shore up her mind.

But she especially needed to stop sighing like a love-struck teenager.

It was time for Isabella to woman-up and get her man back.

Even if she had to hire him to cater a wedding that was never going to happen.

●

THREE

Henry

HE WAVED as Allie jumped out of the car and then headed up to the front door of the main house at Roosevelt Ranch.

Yup, he'd said main house.

His best friend growing up had done well when she'd married Justin Roosevelt. While the former army medic might come across as unassuming and normal, his family definitely was *not*.

The Roosevelts were richer than Croesus and way above the typical Darlington pay grade, but Justin didn't care about his family's money. In fact, he'd only recently stepped in to help his father with some of the business after discharging from the military.

His focus was his family and supporting Kelly as she lived her dream of running *the* premier horse breeding operation in the States.

Roosevelt Ranch was the perfect place for that.

Kel had practically grown up on the ranch—before it had

gained its current namesake. She'd always been horse crazy and had worked her way into free lessons.

Now she had a set of stables that were so impressive and luxurious they nearly rivaled the main house.

The huge front door opened, and his friend patted Allie's head as she bustled inside, but when he waved and would have driven away, Kel shook her head, taking a step toward him. And considering she had a twin in each arm, Henry knew he was trapped. He'd wait—*no* he'd get out of the car and go to Kelly before she tripped and injured herself or one of the kiddoes on the gravel drive. He'd do it because he was a soft-hearted sucker who often got caught in women's webs and—

Fuck.

He turned off the ignition, popped his door, and got out of his car.

"Hey," he said, slamming it and walking over to her. He slid Jessie from her arms, cuddling the little girl close. Her vibrant green eyes were sleepy. "Did you just wake up from a nap?" he murmured, and she cuddled closer.

"Rocket ship," she said.

Kel laughed.

And speaking of getting caught in a female's webs.

Jessie had him wrapped up tightly in hers. Not that her brother, Jax, didn't have him just as snared.

Henry liked kids.

Always had. Always would.

And since he didn't and probably never would have any of his own, he had no problem being the fun uncle.

"Rocket ship!" Jax said, raising his head up from his mom's shoulder.

"Not so sleepy anymore, are you?" Kelly said with a laugh.

"Rocket ship!" Jessie said again, much more enthusiastically and thus, confirming her mom's statement.

Kel glanced at Henry. He shrugged.

"Okay, two rocket ships each and then you need to go find daddy and bug him for letting you fall asleep." She shook her head. "Goodness knows what this late nap is going to do to your bedtime."

"It's summer," Henry said with a shrug.

"Yes, it is," Kel agreed. "But that doesn't mean bedtime doesn't need to happen."

"Ah, to be a parent."

She smacked him, and he stepped back to prepare Jessie for her first rocket ship.

"Don't hit, Mama," Jax said.

Henry's lips twitched. "Yeah. Don't hit."

She glared, but he ignored it as he dangled Jessie's feet just off the ground, shaking her gently like a rocket ship engine's flaring to life. They counted down together. "Five . . . four . . . three . . . two . . . one!" And she blasted off.

Or rather, he tossed her high into the air, caught her, and then flew the Jessie rocket ship back and forth over the path before landing her safely in front of Jax and Kel.

Jax immediately wiggled his way out of Kel's arms. "My turn!"

Henry obliged and was sweating by the time he finished the four rounds. He waved as the kids ran off to find Justin, heart swelling when they stopped mid-sprint then turned around and threw their little arms around his waist.

"Wuv you!" Jessie said and ran off.

"Wuv you!" Jax parroted, following her.

This was why he'd never moved back to New York. He'd gone for an adventure, to be someone important and famous in the restaurant world, and to make a boatload of money. He'd done it, too, made the money, had begun to be *somebody* in certain high circles, and then . . . his dad had gotten sick.

And he'd discovered that being a part of this circle was so much more valuable.

"So," Kel said. "Cobb salad?"

Or not.

He turned. "I've got to get back to the restaurant."

Kel caught his arm. "Is this about the beautiful brunette with the Italian accent?"

"How do you know about Isabella?" He'd rotated back to face her before realizing his mistake. She'd called his bluff, and he'd caved.

Kel's smile was beatific. She swept a hand around them. "This is Darlington, remember? Plus, she's staying at the B&B, and certain key people saw her walk into your restaurant the other day." He groaned, but she ignored him. "And then this morning, you're making a Cobb salad that no one ordered. Melissa checked and told me, and we put two and two together. So *she's* the reason Cobb salads are anathema? Why? Did you know her back in New York?"

He sighed, somehow following all of that and knowing that if he didn't give her some details she'd hound him until the dogs came home, no pun intended. "Yes."

There. That ought to be enough.

"Yes?" She raised a brow. "Just *yes?* Seriously?"

"Bye, Kel." This time when he turned for his car, he got his ass in gear and didn't stop, not even when she huffed and he heard her footsteps on the gravel behind him.

"Henry," she began, hand on his arm.

He brushed it off. "Leave it, Kel. Please."

"I—"

He was saved by a loud crash, followed by crying from inside the house. He stopped, gestured inside. "Go."

Kel glared, but she was already hustling toward the noise. "This isn't over," she called as she reached the front door.

Yeah, that was exactly what he was afraid of.

FOUR

Isabella

SHE CLOSED her laptop with a disgusted sigh. Her bank account was pathetic . . . as in pathetically empty.

Her father had acknowledged her disobedience by cutting her off. Which she'd known would happen, of course. No one crossed Roberto Mariano, most especially not some helpless female creature.

Isabella groaned then pushed herself to her feet and forced herself to take stock. Her bank account had just over a thousand dollars in it, and while her father considered the amount a pittance, she knew how to make it stretch.

She'd done it before in New York.

She'd make it work this time around as well.

Her first step was to get out of the bed and breakfast because who knew how long her credit card would work—

Isabella's stomach growled with a vengeance.

Okay, so her *first* order of business was to get some food into her belly. Then to get out of the bed and breakfast and into something cheaper . . . and hopefully more permanent.

Because she wasn't leaving without Henry.

Feeling slightly less depressed, she picked up her purse and left the room.

That mild buoyant feeling lasted the three minutes it took for her to descend one flight of stairs, cross the quaint two-lane road, and push through the diner's doors on the other side.

More than a dozen eyes turned in her direction, narrowed, and then flicked away, the small town's version of a cold shoulder.

Isabella didn't have to be a rocket scientist—and she most definitely wasn't smart enough to delve into aeronautics—to know that.

Less than twenty-four hours and word had gotten around.

She remembered Henry talking about the town gossip train, explaining that something would happen in the morning and by the afternoon, every person in Darlington would be able to recite the details verbatim. But she had thought he exaggerated. Isabella was from a small town herself and aside from a few interfering grannies, most people kept to themselves.

She decided she rather preferred *that* option. Especially when faced with the onslaught of narrowed lids and subsequent dismissal.

Click.

The noise made her jump, her gaze darting from left to right before finally catching a flash of movement in front of her.

An elderly woman wearing a purple sweatshirt with a pair of kittens on its front stood in front of her, the latest model i-whatever in her hand. When Isabella's eyes met hers, she lowered the phone and smiled up at her.

It was unnerving, that smile.

As though the little old lady with tufts of curly white hair could see straight into her soul.

This would be the point that Isabella's grandmother would

cross herself and pray to the Holy Ghost for protection, but Isabella herself had never been much for religion or the old ways or—

And now she was sad.

A hand slid into hers, making her jump for the second time in as many minutes.

"Come with me, dear," the woman said, tugging her in the direction of a booth. "I'm Esther."

"I'm Isabella," she said and started to dig in her heels. Based on Henry's reaction when she'd walked in before and that of the current patrons dining, she'd made a mistake coming here. She should leave before she caused a scene.

And what was that about fighting for Henry? her conscience reminded her.

Well, she wasn't exactly anticipating it being so . . . public.

She knew she had a mountain to climb and so many things to explain, but—

Fine. She was a fucking coward.

"I should go," she began.

Esther gave a surprisingly strong tug for a woman her size. "You need to eat something, girlie. You're practically skin and bones."

Her father saying the same thing would have hurt Isabella's feelings. Then again, his words were always a critique, definitely not said with the same sort of exasperated tone as Esther's —as though she were a naughty child rather than solely a source of disappointment.

Plus, the diner smelled wonderful.

Sweet laced with savory, the remnants of breakfast trailing into lunch and even an early dinner. The heavy note of fried food mixed with something that made her mouth water. Tangy, spicy . . . sultry.

Henry's food.

Her stomach rumbled just as Esther pushed her down into a booth.

"See?" she said. "You're hungry and need to eat."

Isabella nodded and relinquished the battle she was losing anyway. Plus, Esther was the one person who didn't seem to hate her, so she'd be wise to not alienate a potential ally. "Yes, you're right."

Esther nodded. "Of course, I am."

Isabella smiled and picked up the menu the woman shoved in her direction. "What do you like to order here?"

"Oh, I'm boring and always get the same thing." She waved a hand. "Can I call you Bella?"

Her heart skipped a beat. Only one other person in the world had called her Bella . . . and he was the person this restaurant was named after. "Um, sure," she said and picked up the menu that lay on the scarred tabletop. "What's the same thing?"

The strands of jeweled necklaces that hung around Esther's neck tinkled as she tilted her head. "What *same thing?*"

Isabella smiled. "What's the dish you always order?"

"A fried chicken sandwich with a side of Brussels sprouts."

Except the explanation hadn't come from Esther.

Isabella glanced up and saw a very annoyed Henry standing at the end of the table, a plate in one hand.

"Sounds delicious," she murmured.

Esther lifted a plastic glass of water to her mouth, two wedges of lemon bobbing in the cup, and took a long swallow. "It's the best thing on the menu."

"I'd better order one then," Isabella said.

"No," Henry snapped, his tone harsher than she'd ever heard before.

Isabella's shoulders came up, protecting herself against the onslaught that was certain to come.

She froze and waited.

Then waited some more because the verbal onslaught never actually came. So great, she was sitting there in a restaurant full of people who were pretending to ignore her, but in actuality were probably watching her like a hawk so they could talk about her later, with her shoulders up around her ears and her spine bowed like a pathetic ring-hoarding creature.

"I—" she began, forcing herself to straighten.

"Bella is hungry," Esther interrupted, patting her on the hand. "We'll share the sandwich until you can bring out another one." She preempted Isabella's argument by picking up her knife and cutting the sandwich in half. "Bring an extra plate, dear," she told Henry then speared a Brussels sprout on her fork and held it up. "Try this, Bella. You'll never have a tastier vegetable."

Isabella took the fork and bit into the green sphere.

In an instant, flavors burst to life on her tongue.

Salt and pepper. Oil and smoke. A light sweetness trailed by a depth of earthiness. Her eyes widened as she chewed, the slight crunch of the outer leaves giving way to a smooth center.

She swallowed, forcing herself to smile in Esther's direction and all too aware of Henry's heavy gaze on her.

After wiping her mouth with a napkin, she dared sneak a glance in his direction.

His eyes were unreadable, but she thought that she might detect hope in the pale blue depths. Or if not that, then perhaps they were empty of anger.

"It is the most delicious vegetable I've ever eaten," she said, sincerely feeling that.

For some reason, that seemed to make him furious. His eyes flashed, and he glared down at her for a moment before pushing the plate back an inch so it was closer to Esther. "Eat," he told her. "Before it gets cold. I'll make Isabella something."

And then he was gone, striding across the floor, pushing through the pair of swinging doors with circular windows.

Walking away from her when there was so much to say.

Well, if that wasn't a role reversal, then Isabella didn't know what was.

"What happened between you two?" Esther asked between bites of sandwich.

Isabella froze for a heartbeat before telling the truth. "I messed up."

"Well, that much is clear, dear, but I want to know all the juicy details for the town's Snapchat." She pulled out her phone. "Do you want sparkling sunglasses or a unicorn horn?"

"I—" Isabella shook her head, the words not computing. "Um . . ."

"Unicorn horn," Esther said with a nod. "Good choice."

And then, before Isabella could stop her, she found herself the object of Esther's cell phone's camera.

"Tell us, dear, how you broke our Henry's heart . . "

Which was the exact moment she decided that coming to the diner had been a huge mistake, no matter how tasty the Brussels sprouts.

FIVE

Henry

HE WAS GOING to kill Esther.

Or at the very least rip her cell phone from her old, wily hands and launch it straight into the trash can.

Isabella's cheeks were bright red, her shoulders curved up as though to form a shield, and Henry spared a thought for what had happened to the cheerful, confident woman she'd been back in New York.

Fearless. Never at a loss for words.

But she didn't look fearless now.

She looked mortified and panicked and, *fuck it all*, he couldn't stop himself from rescuing her.

Sucker that made him.

He set the bag of food he'd boxed up for her on the table, having intended to feed her as requested by Esther while getting her out of sight, as his heart demanded, and wrapped his hand around her elbow.

Then he snagged the cell from Esther, turned it off, and tugged Isabella from the booth.

"I need to borrow you."

"Hen—" Esther began, a complaint about him ruining her fun no doubt on the tip of her tongue.

"Meal's on the house today," he told her and snatched the bag of food before leading Isabella through the double doors and into the back of the diner. He bypassed the kitchen on the right, walked past the bathrooms and his office on the left, not stopping until he pushed out into the alley behind the restaurant.

An old wooden bench from his father's days sat along the brick wall.

He pushed her down onto it, shoved the bag of food into her lap, and turned to leave.

Her fingers on the back of his hand stopped him.

It could barely be called contact, the brush of skin to skin was so feather-light, but the force didn't matter. Not when it was Isabella. *Always*, it had been like this. Fire in his veins, lightning strikes contained in a human body, the barest touch and he half-expected to glance down and see himself turned to ash.

But that had been their problem, hadn't it?

They'd burned too hot, flared too quickly.

And in the end, he'd been left with nothing.

He stared into her eyes, a deep brown that had always reminded him of espresso, and she flinched back, eyes tearing away from his, dropping to the ground.

Fuck.

"I'm sorry I didn't come here with you. Back then," she added when he didn't reply. And how *could* he reply? That wound was a horrible, festering thing. It didn't heal.

It *never* healed.

Apologies didn't bring his father back.

And . . . that wasn't Isabella's fault.

She hadn't spent years smoking away her life on that very bench. She hadn't eaten poorly or disregarded doctor's orders.

She just . . . hadn't dropped everything to come home with him.

He'd vilified her for that because it was easier to be mad at her than angry with himself, easier to blame her for not coming when in reality, he felt horrible because *he* hadn't come back sooner.

"I didn't know what else to do," she whispered.

"Yeah," he said. "Me neither. I just knew I needed someone to be there for me."

Her chin dropped to her chest and she nodded.

"It wasn't fair for me to expect that person to be you."

Isabella's eyes shot to his, lips parted in surprise. "I—"

"We were new and hadn't been together long—" He shook his head, tried again. "While I clearly thought we were something more . . . permanent, it wasn't fair for me to expect you to feel the same—"

She pushed to her feet. "Henry—"

God, he loved when she said his name, a soft 'h,' a slightly rolled 'r'—

"It wasn't like that. I *loved* you. I just . . . had to go."

"Why?"

Why then? Why when he needed her? Why, when for the first time in his life he'd asked a woman to stay, had she gone?

She shook her head, clutched the bag of food to her chest. "I should have stayed. Should have told you—"

Breaking off with another shake of her head, she stepped closer to him.

Close enough for him to smell her, close enough for the breeze to flit her ponytail forward and for the soft tendrils to tease his cheek, close enough for him to remember exactly how good it had been between them.

"Tell me what?" he asked.

She bit her lip.

"Bella." He used his old nickname. He shouldn't have. It was too familiar, but, fuck it, he *was* familiar with Isabella. Henry knew how quickly she could chop an onion, knew she could make him really fucking delicious pasta with a recipe that was more touch than measurements. He knew the sound she made when he kissed her properly, could perfectly recall the feel of her beneath him.

He knew this woman in the depths of his soul.

"Henry," she murmured and stepped closer.

The back door flew open, would have cracked her in the head if Henry hadn't managed to catch it.

A man emerged, tall, dark, and movie star handsome. While Henry was confident enough in himself to recognize the other man as objectively attractive, he also immediately disliked him. His teeth were too white, his facial hair too groomed, his pale pink linen suit like he was trying too hard. And his knee jerk reaction was warranted, Henry thought, because the man immediately took Bella into his arms and kissed her long enough that he had to look away, a red haze filling his vision.

This wasn't his woman.

It didn't matter who kissed her.

"Isabella," the man said and while Henry had been expecting an Italian accent to match Bella's, his was strictly American. "I've come, my darling. Where's this ranch that you talked about for the wedding?" He turned to Henry, whose gaze had jumped to the couple at the mention of the ranch. "You must be the caterer? My Isa mentioned this place." He glanced down at the bag in Isabella's hands. "Oh, darling, did you get some samples to try? We should go back to the room and *sample* them."

Henry shuddered at the connotation imparted in that word and started to turn back for the diner.

He caught sight of Bella's face as he did so.

The man had taken the bag from her, was running his free hand through her ponytail.

And she looked absolutely miserable.

Not his problem.

"Isa, darling . . ."

She cringed, and he remembered how much she hated being called Isa.

"I've missed you."

Not. His. Problem.

She extracted herself. "Sergio."

The man's eyes had been focused on Bella's breasts. The sharp tone had his gaze flying up to meet hers.

"Yes, darling?"

"I need you . . ." Her stare flicked to Henry's then away. "I need to talk to you. Alone."

Inexplicably, a giant boulder dropped into Henry's gut, stealing his breath.

For a moment, he'd thought she was going to tell Sergio, "*I need you to go.*"

Insane.

Delusional.

Some other adjective Henry wasn't going to search his brain for. Because it didn't matter. Clearly he'd lost his mind. She wasn't miserable. She was about to get married.

He turned, caught the door handle, and tugged it open.

Isabella's voice stopped him on the threshold. "Henry?"

"Yeah?" he asked, not turning to face her. His pulse sped while an unbidden, and decidedly unwanted, thread of hope wove into his heart. But still Henry didn't turn, unwilling to risk seeing a dismissal in her expression. Not again.

"Thanks for the food."

He was really glad he couldn't see her face.

"Sure," he said, tone somehow casual as he let the door close behind him.

And that panel slamming shut was the perfect end to the most painful chapter of his life.

Good riddance.

SIX

Isabella

SERGIO GRABBED HER ARM. "Let's go," he gritted out.

"No." She yanked free, stepped back when he would have grabbed her again. "I already told you. I'm *not* marrying you."

Black brows drew together. "That's not what your father—"

Fuck. They'd had this conversation so many times. Her father didn't get to decide every single detail of her life, and he sure as hell wasn't going to choose the man she was going to marry. She'd been weak when she had accepted Sergio's proposal in the first place, mostly because she'd thought Sergio actually loved her, that she would grow to love him in return.

Because what Isabella wanted most in the world was to be part of a family.

By blood wasn't even a requirement because she'd learned over the years that shared DNA didn't always mean love and respect were present. She'd adopt or have babies, make friends who liked her for herself. She'd have Sergio, whom she didn't love, but perhaps her affection for him might develop into that one day.

And then she would finally be happy.

Except things didn't work out that way.

"My father is not me," she said.

"He promised."

There.

There was the hard edge that Sergio had been so careful to hide from her at first. He'd been so perfect, pretending to really care about what she was saying and feeling, responding with all the right things. He'd charmed her father and that didn't often happen, but then again what her father wanted most in the world was a son.

One daughter. No sons.

His everlasting disappointment.

Things might have been better if she'd been interested in the family business, but investments and stocks made her eyes glaze over, the same as her waxing poetic about olive oil did to her father.

They'd agreed tacitly to not discuss their mutual interests.

Which had been for the best, and everything had been great for the two years she'd spent in New York.

Until her father decided that her playtime was up.

Until *she* decided that she wanted to be with Henry, not the man her father had picked for her.

That man hadn't been Sergio. No, Sergio was the last in a long line of *respectable* men her father had chosen—which meant they were good at business and would carry on the mantle of MR Investments respectably when her father passed and would give him reasonably attractive grandbabies.

What it *didn't* mean was that they were kind or loving or gave two shits about her.

Most had looked right through her or treated her with near disdain while sidling close to her father, but fortunately, they'd all also eventually pissed him off. Thus, the pressure to marry them had passed and they were discarded as easily as a used tissue. But there was always another man.

Another man to care more about her father and the business than her.

She was the enticing little bow on top.

Until Sergio.

He'd played the game right, had managed to not piss her father off while also manipulating her.

She had been such a fool.

"You're coming home," Sergio said through gritted teeth. "I didn't put in all this time to just let you go."

She snatched the bag of food from his hands. "*You* should go home," she said. "I'm done dancing to my father's tune. I don't love you. I never have. I'm not—"

One second, she was glaring up at him, the next she was pinned against the brick wall, his hand around her throat. "I don't give a fuck whether you love me or not. Your father will cut me out of the business unless you come home and marry me. So you're going to shut up and—"

Isabella didn't think, just reacted.

Her knee came up hard, hitting him squarely in the groin.

Sergio collapsed to the ground.

Unfortunately, the hand around her neck didn't release, and she found herself dragged down alongside him, unable to break her fall. Her side collided with the concrete first, and she felt the thin silk of her shirt tear, her skin beneath it burn. The next to hit was her hip and finally her head, which made her bite her tongue and her mouth fill with blood.

One hard tug and she managed to extricate herself, rolling gingerly to her feet and picking up the now-mangled bag of food from the ground.

"Go home, Sergio. Leave me to my life."

He only groaned in response. Relieved that he didn't seem

to be in any shape to come after her again, Isabella hurried out of the alley. Luckily, there were a few napkins in the bag, and she grabbed one out as she hobbled around to the front of the diner.

She was ashamed to say tears were running down her cheeks. That, along with her entire body hurting and the sharp tang of iron in her mouth, and she wasn't the most together she'd ever been in her life.

Especially when Sergio shouted her name and staggered out from the alley.

"Isabella, I'm not—"

She limped on, wanting to make it across the street and into the bed and breakfast. She'd left her phone, but maybe the girl at the front desk could—

She waited for a car to pass before crossing the road, but when she glanced back Sergio seemed to have regained himself. He was hurrying after her with only the slightest hitch in his step and gaining on her quickly.

The car that had driven by her stopped, but Isabella barely heard it in her effort to put as much distance between herself and Sergio.

Instead, what she *did* hear were footsteps closing in and Sergio's annoyed grunts.

She couldn't let him catch her.

Instinctively, she knew that. He'd been irritated before she'd kneed him, and that had resulted in him tossing her against a wall and choking her.

If he caught her now?

Bella shuddered to think.

She moved faster.

The door to the bed and breakfast was just feet away, and Isabella lunged for it only to have her head jerked back roughly as Sergio caught her ponytail.

Which was the exact moment she heard something else.

A deep male voice.

"Let her go and step back." Her eyes darted to the right, and she had never been more relieved in her life to see a police officer. He wore a deep blue uniform and approached them slowly. "*I said* to let her go." Icy steel in his words.

Sergio released her hair, and she hurried to put some space between them.

"Someone want to tell me what the hell is going on?"

Bella found it almost impossible to push words past her now-aching throat, and before she managed, Sergio chimed in, sounding sickeningly nonchalant.

"My fiancée and I are just having a little disagreement."

"I'm not his fiancée," she managed.

"Then why are you wearing my ring, darling?" he asked sweetly.

She'd considered pawning it, that was why. However, in that moment she didn't give a damn about any money it might bring her. She yanked it off, flung it on the ground. "I'm not his fiancée anymore."

"And you like beating up women who *used* to be your fiancée?" the officer said just as a squad car roared up the street beside them, lights flashing.

"She merely had a bad fall."

One black brow went up. "She fell, and you caught her by yanking her hair out of her head?"

Sergio shrugged. "Her hair got caught on my watch."

"Hmm."

Sergio shifted like he was going to move toward her, and the officer caught his arm. "Have a seat over here," he ordered, tugging Sergio down onto the curb a good ten feet away from her.

Isabella blinked, wavering on her feet, but a strong hand caught her.

"Easy now," Esther said, steadying her.

The doors opened on the other squad car, and a female deputy got out. She was short with a tight blonde ponytail and kind eyes. "Rob?" she asked, glancing between Isabella and Sergio.

"Domestic disturbance," he replied. "Would you mind taking her statement?" He hesitated before adding, "Maybe somewhere she can sit down?"

The woman nodded.

"Thanks, Pam."

Another nod before the woman crossed over to Isabella. "Hi," she said. "I'm Officer Harting, but you can call me Pam."

"H-hi," Isabella said then lifted her chin and forced her voice to steady. "Did you want to go inside so we can talk?"

"That would be good."

Isabella nodded and patted Esther's hand. "Thank you. I'm fine now."

Esther glared up at her before extracting several tissues from her fanny pack, "You're bleeding all over that pretty shirt of yours." She pressed them to Bella's arm.

"Oh!" Bella's eyes shot to the spot, and she saw the blood dripping down her fingertips. Damn. She must be cut deeper than she realized.

Officer Harting held up a black rectangular-shaped bag. "I've got her covered, Esther."

"Good."

The older woman stayed where she was.

"This is not going on the town's Facebook page."

Esther rolled her eyes. "Clearly not," she said, and Officer Harting's formal stance relaxed slightly. At least until she said, "It's much more fitting for Snapchat."

Somehow, Bella felt her lips twitch.

And honestly, it was nice to feel something aside from terror or numbness.

She'd seen the sharp edge of Sergio's temper just once before . . . and had the scar to prove it.

It had been the final straw, the piece that had given her the courage to leave.

But somehow, she'd almost convinced herself that she'd imagined the entire thing. That he hadn't actually hit her that night after the benefit, that she *had* been a little too tipsy and tripped down the final few stairs. That he hadn't been furious with her moments before it happened for embarrassing him.

Because she'd had an opinion that didn't agree with his.

Because she was supposed to be seen and not heard.

Even though he'd convinced her that he was a nice guy and actually liked hearing her opinions.

Just not when they contradicted his. Or in public when she was playing the role of arm candy. Or, preferably, that she'd just shut the fuck up and do what he said.

Esther stomped her foot, making Bella jump. "Look at her. She's half stunned. She needs a hospital, not an interrogation."

Bella shook her head and winced when the movement made her head ache even more. "I'm fine," she said. "I just need to sit down for a few minutes and eat something. I slept through breakfast and got in too late for much of a dinner last night."

Esther tsked. "You're already too skinny as it is."

The admonishment made Isabella smile, but when she glanced up at Officer Harting, the other woman looked concerned. She held up her finger. "Can you follow this?" she asked, moving it side to side.

"I'm not concussed, I—" Except just tracking the digit made Bella's brain feel like it was going to burst out of her skull.

"See?" Esther said. "Not fine."

"I'll wrap her arm and drive her to the ED."

"Oh, no. I'm—" Bella started to shake her head again and stopped with another wince. She really needed to stop doing that.

"No arguments," Officer Harting said. "You need to be cleared medically before I can take your statement." She made short work of wrapping Bella's arm then led her over to the front seat of the squad car. "Take it slow now."

Considering the amount of pain coursing through her body at the moment, slow wasn't a problem.

Officer Harting reached over her and buckled Isabella's seat belt before she could reach for it then softly closed the door. Bella watched through the windshield as the female cop moved across the road and spoke to Rob—at least she'd thought she'd heard that was his name—for a few moments then got back into the car. Just as Officer Harting had started up the engine, another police cruiser drove up, but she just waved and clicked the transmission into drive.

"Thank you, Officer Harting," Isabella said.

"Just doing my job." A shrug as she tossed Bella a smile, pale green eyes twinkling in the late afternoon sunlight. "And call me Pam, please. All that Officer Harting stuff gets really tiring."

Bella's lips twitched. "Pam. Thank you."

"Does he have a history of violence toward you?" The question was quiet in volume, but deadly in tone.

"No," Isabella denied immediately and then was forced to qualify her statement nearly as quickly. "Only once before. I thought—I didn't think he'd follow me here."

Officer—*Pam*—nodded grimly.

"I'm not the kind of woman to stand by and let someone hurt me." Except, hadn't she done just that? *No, dammit.* She'd fought back. Both times she'd fought back.

"You don't strike me as such."

Bella lifted her chin. "I'm not."

Pam nodded. "I believe you." A beat before, "Why don't you close your eyes and relax? It's a twenty-minute drive to the hospital."

"I'm—" Her gaze caught on movement outside of the car.

Henry slammed through the diner's door, skidding to a stop when he saw her in the front seat of the police cruiser, jaw dropping open, hand extending toward her.

Bella closed her eyes, blinking against the burn of tears.

She couldn't face him.

Not now.

Maybe not ever.

SEVEN

Henry

TILLY CAME UP BESIDE HIM. "You should go."

"What?" Henry blinked, clearing away the image of the blood on Isabella's pale face. Bright red and so much of it that it had covered her from temple to jaw bone.

He never should have left her in that alley.

"You should go after her," Tilly said again. "Frank and I can handle the kitchen."

"I—" He shook his head, tried for a second time. "I should stay and—"

Tilly sighed, hazel eyes taking on the slightest bit of disappointment. "Henry," she said. "Like it or not, she's yours, and you know you'll never forgive yourself if you don't go after her."

He dropped his chin to his chest, knew she was right. Like it or not, some part of him would always belong to Isabella. "Will you show Rob the security footage? There's a camera in the alley." He handed her the key to his office, where the cameras' hard drives were stored.

Tilly nodded. "Of course."

With that, he hustled over to his car and drove to the hospital. By the time he pushed through the doors to the emergency department, Isabella had already been taken into the back, but he did manage to flag down Melissa's friend, Haley, who promised to come and get him when Bella was ready for visitors.

And then he waited.

A familiar feeling when it came to this woman, though this situation was totally unique.

Rob texted him around an hour in, telling him he'd reviewed the footage and would be taking the hard drive it was backed up on.

Henry thanked him then tried and failed to hold back his question.

What did it show?

Rob's reply came a second later.

You know I can't tell you that.

Henry sighed.

Yeah, I know.

His phone buzzed.

Just know that he's a bastard and your girl fought back.

There was that phrase again, the whole of Darlington assuming that Bella was his. It was presumptuous and patently untrue, but then he thought of that asshole Sergio kissing her and worse, of him hurting Bella, and Henry knew that he'd never be able to affect disinterest.

Isabella was inside of him, woven deep and knotted tightly, and he'd never had any chance in Hell of excising her.

Not then. Not now. Not ever.

Haley waved him over to the counter. "She'll need to be admitted overnight. She has a slight brain hemorrhage—"

"*What?*" His gut clenched. Fuck, why had he left her alone with that bastard?

Haley touched his hand. "She's going to be okay. It's minor, and they're treating it with medication. Dr. Hamilton doesn't think she'll need surgery."

Medication. Doesn't think. Surgery. Henry's mind spun.

"Look," she said. "Isabella will be fine. She's conscious and her pain is under control. She . . ." Haley bit her lip. "She also asked me to tell you to go home."

Henry glared at her. "How does she even know I'm here?"

"Don't take that tone with me, Henry Miller. Lest you forget, I hauled your ass home once after you tossed your cookies in Mrs. Davidson's class, or did you forget?" Crossed arms, a narrow-eyed glare. "Do you *want* me to remind the town that your nickname for a time was Henry the Spewer? Because I still have the pictures."

Jesus.

This woman was insane.

"I am *not* insane," Haley snapped, and Henry could have kicked himself for being so off his game he'd said that aloud. "I'm protecting my patient. She told me I could give you the very basic details because she knew that you were stubborn enough to not leave without a modicum of assurance. And that's it. Legally, I'm required to safeguard her privacy."

"Hay." He sighed. "I can't just leave it at that—"

She shook her head. "I'm *legally* bound to follow her wishes. You're not her husband or even her emergency contact. And we both know that you definitely don't have power of attorney—"

"Fuck," he muttered, turning away and thrusting his hand through his hair.

"But—" her voice gentled softly. "I *do* know that the door to the department is undergoing maintenance and that it's not currently locked." He whirled around, hope springing to life. "And that she's in exam room four, at least until she gets moved upstairs."

Henry crossed over to Haley, gripped her by the shoulders, and kissed her cheek. "Thank you."

She waved him off. "Just don't be an asshole and make me regret my moment of weakness."

He nodded, hurrying over to the door Haley had indicated and slipping through. Luckily the waiting room was empty aside from him, their small county hospital rarely busy, especially in the early evening on a weekday. He checked the signs, following them until he found room four, and knocked quietly on the closed door.

"Come in," came Bella's voice, and Henry's heart hurt all over again to hear it rasp through the wooden panel. He was going to kill the bastard.

What kind of fucking name was Sergio anyway?

A sexy Italian one that Isabella had apparently wanted to marry.

Fuck.

"Hello?" she called louder. "You can come in."

Henry sighed, tried to focus and calm emotions that had been roiling like a pot about to boil over since Bella had reappeared in town.

Twenty-four hours.

Was that all it had been? It felt like a lifetime, like too much had changed for it to have only been one day.

"Enough," he muttered, forcing himself to focus as he pushed through the door.

Then almost went right back outside so he could hunt Sergio down and tear him to shreds. The side of her face was scraped up, and bruises had already begun to form on her cheekbone and around her eye. Her arm was bandaged, and an ice pack was positioned on her right hip.

He'd let that happen.

Her gaze dropped to the bed, but not before he saw shame cross her expression.

And, didn't she see? She didn't have a single thing to feel ashamed about. It was all on the fucking scum of the earth that was Sergio. It was on *Henry* for not recognizing the bastard for what he was, for not protecting her, for leaving her and—

"Why are you here?"

The ice in her tone made him smile. Somehow, it made him smile.

Because it reminded him of the first time he'd laid eyes on her.

She was the assistant pastry chef in his friend's restaurant, and he'd come in to meet Brian for an early lunch and to compare their thoughts on a local farm that wanted to sell its produce in gourmet New York eateries.

He hadn't been impressed with the produce, but he *had* been mesmerized by Isabella Mariano.

Irritated by his interruption, beautiful eyes sparking fire at him when he'd dared asked for a taste of the gelato she'd just taken out of the ice cream machine. She'd tossed her ponytail over one shoulder, huffed as she scooped some of the concoction into a bowl and all but tossed it at him.

Lavender and honey and his taste buds—and quite frankly— his heart had never recovered

She'd been fire tempered by frost, and he'd fallen headfirst for her.

And he *still* couldn't remember a single word from that meeting with Brian.

But the texture of that gelato, the way the flavors had exploded on his tongue, *that* he could remember.

"Hi," he said, tucking the memory safely away and moving to take the chair at her bedside. He forced lightness into his tone. "You look like you tangled with a very aggressive stand mixer and barely lived to tell the tale."

Her glare had been epic, but the mention of the stand mixer saved him.

Or at least he pretended it did.

Because her lips curved into a small smile and she glanced up at him. "Remember the cooking class?"

"When the so-called expert didn't know how to secure the attachment and it flew through the kitchen?" He grinned. "How could I possibly forget?"

Bella touched her uninjured cheek, the faintest white line visible. "It was the first time I had to have my face glued together. I didn't even know that was a thing." Her smile faded, and she shifted uncomfortably on the bed. "Apparently, I'm making it a regular occurrence."

"Is your hip hurting you?" He reached for the ice pack, intending to adjust it.

"I'm fine."

He raised a brow. "Reminiscing about Super Glue aside, you're definitely not fine. I mean, look at you—"

The wrong words.

Henry realized that exactly a heartbeat too late.

As in, they'd already crossed his lips, and the damage had been done.

Bella's face fell, any trace of amusement in her espresso eyes disappearing.

"I didn't mean it like that."

"I know." She started to shrug, broke off with a wince.

And silence.

"Bella, sweetheart, I'm sorry."

Her gaze flew to his, shock loosening her words. "What could *you* possibly have to be sorry for?"

"I shouldn't have left you alone." He caught the ice pack when she gingerly shifted in his direction. "I could tell you were uncomfortable, and I was so wrapped up in my own feelings that I—"

"Henry." She rested her palm on top of his. He hadn't even realized he'd been gripping the railing of the bed. "I left you, remember? You have nothing to be sorry about."

There was something in her tone that prickled on the edge of his consciousness, but before he could tug at the thought, she let go of his hand.

The contact shouldn't have made a difference.

It was the barest touch of skin against skin.

And yet, its absence was almost painful.

"You should go," she said, turning her head away. "I think that nice nurse already told you that much."

"Haley did try to give me the brush off."

Bella pressed her lips tightly together then grumbled, "Didn't work, apparently."

"No," Henry said, biting back a smile. "It didn't."

She huffed, not looking at him.

"And I already called Anastasia at the bed and breakfast," he announced. "She packed up your stuff for you and dropped it by my house."

Bella stared at him, mouth open in surprise.

"Is there anything you really need? Medication? A phone charger?"

Her teeth clacked together. "No," she gritted out.

"Okay, great." Henry crossed one ankle over the other. "So,

we can just hang out and catch up."

"Catch. Up?"

"Yeah," he said. "Isn't that why you came back in the first place? You wanted to reconnect?"

"I—"

"I know I've wondered what you've been up to these last five years."

"It's—" Her jaw worked for a long moment. "We're not old friends, Henry. We parted on . . . " Bella trailed off.

"Bad terms?" he asked, feeling way more casual than he actually felt. "You could say that."

"I'm—you didn't even want to talk to me yesterday."

He leaned back in his chair. "Things are different today."

"Because Sergio hurt me?"

"Yeah."

She scowled.

"But also because I've never stopped thinking about you, Isabella."

She froze, presumably in shock, and though his casual position didn't change, Henry definitely didn't feel anywhere *near* casual about the statement that had just crossed his lips.

Maybe he'd thought it and maybe deep down he'd known it was the truth, but Henry hadn't planned on exposing himself to Bella, not when her betrayal was still so raw. Five years hadn't made the sight of her walking away from him disappear from his mind. Five years didn't erase the painful memories of nursing a broken heart, a dying father, and a devastated mother.

Five years didn't make the past go away.

But five years without Bella had taught him things, too.

He didn't want more years without her. He wanted more time *with* her.

She'd just opened her mouth to reply when there was a knock and the door swung open.

Haley popped her head in. "They're all ready for you upstairs," she announced cheerfully before pausing and glancing between them. "Everything okay in here?"

"We're fine," Bella said before Henry could order Haley to go right back out that door and not come back until Bella had told him what she'd been about to say.

"Good," Haley said then ignored him completely as she crossed over to the gurney. She unlocked the wheels, pulled the bags attached to Bella's IV off the pole and set them on the bed next to her. "Let's get you upstairs then and settled. The doctor ordered another CT to see about the hemorrhage, so no food until that reads clear, I'm sorry to say."

Bella groaned. "I don't think I could ever be one of those girls who fasts or even goes on a diet. The hunger is worse than the headache and dizziness. Henry," she said, seeming to suddenly remember he was still there. "You should go home and sleep."

He ignored that, rising from the chair.

"My guess is that you'll be able to have breakfast in the morning," Haley said and started to push the gurney out into the hall. "Tonight you'll rest, and we'll make sure you're on your way to recovery." She paused, glanced back at Henry, her expression decidedly leaning toward *well, are you coming?*

Oh, Henry was definitely coming.

He wasn't leaving his woman alone.

Not ever again.

EIGHT

Isabella

THE NICE NURSE, Haley, had lied.

Her night wasn't restful, not in the least.

She was poked and prodded all night, as the nurses checked all the regular vital signs—blood pressure, temperature, oxygen levels—but also were constantly monitoring her brain.

Not exactly comforting knowing she'd somehow managed to hit her head in the exact right way to cause a hemorrhage.

A hemorrhage that barely warranted the name, according to the neurologist who'd come in to check on her around midnight. She was trying not to freak out about the fact that her brain was bleeding.

But her brain was bleeding!

Still, the doctor had studied her scan then put her through a series of strange exercises before assuring her she would be fine. Of course, the words didn't comfort her so much as the fact that aside from the nagging headache and dizziness, she actually felt better, too.

Her mind wasn't so foggy, and the pain was more migraine level and less her skull was too small for her brain.

Fingers on her cheek startled her.

"How are you feeling?"

Her eyes met Henry's. He hadn't left her side the entire evening, had even followed her down to the CT suite, though the tech had made him wait outside the room.

They hadn't talked much throughout the night and though he'd stayed in the room when Officer Harting—*Pam* had returned to take Bella's statement, he hadn't commented on her side of things.

His expression *had* turned deadly though.

Eventually, Pam had left, but Henry still hadn't spoken much, just watched her through lidded eyes all while studying her with an intensity that made her skin prickle. When she'd finally succumbed to sleep, it had been a welcome relief.

"Hungry," she whispered when his fingers brushed her cheek again.

He smiled, dark circles underneath his eyes. "If your scan is clear, I think breakfast might be on the menu. Though, I'm not sure how good hospital food is."

"I don't care about quality at the moment. I need quantity."

His lips twitched. "*That* I can arrange."

"What time is it?" she asked. Her room overlooked a street light and so the same dimness had filtered through the closed blinds all night, giving her no clue to the time. Then there was the fact that her cell phone was with the rest of her stuff.

At Henry's house.

They needed to talk about that.

Oh boy, did they.

But maybe not right now.

Because she was really freaking hungry.

Henry seemed to read her mind because he pushed out of

the chair he'd been camped in for most of the night and stretched with a quiet groan. "I'll go and see if I can find the nurse. Maybe I can at least rustle you up some Jell-O."

"Oh, my God. That sounds amazing." Her stomach rumbled loudly. "Lime, please. Or at least, any flavor aside from grape."

He chuckled. "Is that your fine palate speaking?"

She grinned, this teasing, smiling Henry she knew, and it made her heart happy. "Absolutely."

He slipped out of the room, returning a few moments later with the nurse who nixed the idea of any food, even Jell-O, until a final scan was complete and read by the neurologist. She did let Bella have a cup of ice, though, along with a tiny container of apple juice. And somehow the little bit of sugar hitting her tongue was the best thing ever.

"I'll get everything moving," the nurse, a pleasant older woman named Alice, told her. "Breakfast is on the horizon."

"I've heard that before," Bella grumbled good-naturedly.

This time the nurse was right. Isabella was scanned, the images read and she was declared to be on the mend by the neurologist, and even a breakfast tray had been delivered to her room, all within two hours.

Lukewarm eggs and floppy bacon had never tasted so good.

She downed the side of sourdough toast, after slapping an obscene amount of butter and jam on it, and it was pretty much the best thing ever. *Ever.*

She was so focused on eating, she even forgot that Henry was in the room.

At least until he wiped a dab of jam from the corner of her mouth. Her breath froze in her lungs, eyes flying up to meet his then trailing down to his lips. He sucked the drop of strawberry sweetness off his thumb, and she would swear to God that she felt that suction on her—

Bella blinked.

She had a brain injury for fuck's sake. Not to mention two stitches on her temple, glue above her eyebrow, and abrasions all down her arm. She was a wreck and . . . Henry was still Henry.

Her body knew his.

Her body remembered how good it had been between them.

She released a shaky breath and picked up another slice of toast, finally remembering her manners. "Do you want it?"

His expression warmed. "No, sweetheart. I might go grab something from the cafeteria and sneak home for a shower though."

Bella bit her lip, knowing she had absolutely no right to want him to stay with her. Hell, she'd told him to go a half dozen times. He had his own life and had already sacrificed more than enough by spending the night with her.

But that didn't change the fact that she'd always felt better when Henry was near.

Mentally, she rolled her eyes at herself.

What had happened to being strong and finding herself?

How was that supposed to be true if she crumpled like a weakling just because she was a little bruised up?

This is hardly a normal situation, her brain—now bleed-free —reminded her.

That didn't change anything.

And great, now she'd gone around in mental circles long enough that Henry was looking at her with concern on his face.

"Of course," she told him. "You should check on the restaurant. I'm sure they're missing you."

"Tuesday is my day off." He frowned. "Are you feeling dizzy again or confused?"

No more than normal.

He grinned as though he'd read the thought in her mind though she knew for a fact that she hadn't spoken aloud.

She *better not* have spoken aloud.

"Get out of here," she ordered. "Go enjoy your day off. Th-thanks for staying. I'll pick up my stuff from your place as soon as possible."

He crossed his arms over his chest. "I'm coming back, Bella. And your stuff can stay at my house however long you need. I only had Anastasia drop it by because she'd told me you intended to check out today, and I didn't want you to have to pay for a night you were in the hospital."

"I—"

Thunderstorms filled his eyes as he glared down at her. "You're not considering going back to that asshole, are you? Is that why you want me to leave?"

"What?" She pushed the table holding the tray of food away from her. "*No.*"

"You were engaged to him."

"*Were* is the key word there," she snapped.

"It didn't seem so key when you asked me to cater your wedding."

Yup.

There was that.

"Henry," she began.

"It's none of my business," he said, holding his hands up, palms facing out. "But if the bastard was willing to do that to you in a public place, I'm terrified to think of what he might do to you in private—"

The blood left her face in a rush, leaving her almost as dizzy as she'd been the night before.

"You already know that, don't you?"

She swallowed. "It's why I left. My father . . . well, he was persistent that I marry Sergio, and I—" She shook her head. "Sergio had me convinced that he loved me."

"What did he do?"

A careful question, and yet Bella easily felt its quiet deadliness. "He showed me he didn't."

Henry dropped his hand onto her thigh, squeezed gently. "That's not an answer."

"It's enough." She blew out a breath. "I left and didn't expect him to follow me. Hell, I'd half-convinced myself the whole thing was an accident. And then in the alley, I thought I'd explain that I didn't want to marry him and he'd leave—"

"I take it he wasn't happy."

"Apparently, my father is threatening to take away his role in the business if he didn't bring me to heel."

"I'm not going back," she added when he didn't say anything. "I won't. I—"

She broke off.

"You what?"

"I wanted to live my life for myself."

Truth.

But not all of it.

She'd left because of Sergio and her father and knowing that she finally needed to find her own way, but she'd come to Darlington, Utah of all places, for a very specific reason.

Henry.

He cupped her unbruised cheek. "You deserve that."

"Why aren't you angry with me anymore?" she blurted, covering his hand with her own when he would have stepped back. "I hurt you. You asked me to come, and I couldn't—"

"I realized that I'd been blaming you for my father's death."

Isabella's heart stopped.

How did he know? How could he possibly know? She'd—

"But I finally got my head out of my ass." Henry slipped his hand free and tugged lightly on a strand of her hair. "My dad had many chances to change his lifestyle. The experimental surgery was successful, and we were beyond lucky that the hospital had a fund for patients in his situation—those who couldn't afford the recommended treatment—because that meant my mom wasn't stuck paying off hundreds of thousands of dollars in medical bills."

Bella began breathing again. He didn't know. His father *had* gotten the treatment.

"But he didn't change after the surgery." Henry sighed. "I loved my dad, but he wasn't much for following orders, even from a medical professional. The second heart attack took him three months after he'd gotten out of rehab."

"I'm so sorry."

He shrugged. "Yeah, me, too. But I felt worse for my mom. She'd thought they'd come through it all and they'd have many more years together. Then boom, he was gone."

"But you lost him, too."

"Yeah," he said with a sigh. "I did."

"And I let you deal with that alone." Bella had gone because she hadn't seen another way, but she still wasn't sure it had been the right thing to do. In the end, it hadn't saved Henry's dad and it had cost her so, so much.

No.

It *had* been the right thing.

She would have known that she hadn't done everything in her power to save Henry's dad. Money meant nothing to her own father, and it had given Henry and his family a chance. She'd been the tradeable commodity in the deal.

So, she'd traded herself for experimental surgeons and fully-paid hospital bills.

In exchange, she'd been the perfect daughter for five years.

But she'd done her time. She wasn't going to marry Sergio, and her father could keep his money.

"I wasn't alone," he said softly.

She was glad for that, would rather it be her who'd been

alone. Hurting, aching, desperate to call him and confess why she'd left. Bella felt that same urge in this moment, to tell him she'd left for noble reasons, but it didn't change the fact that she *had* gone.

She'd sold herself to her father.

Yes, Isabella had chosen it, thinking it was the only thing she could do when she'd discovered that Henry and his family couldn't pay for his father's surgery, but that didn't make it any less shameful.

Especially when it was all for naught.

He'd died anyway.

God, when she'd heard that Henry's dad, Brad, had died, she'd blamed herself. She hadn't chosen the right doctor, hadn't pushed her father for enough money.

But it hadn't been her fault.

And it still didn't change a fucking thing.

She'd left. Henry had lost his dad.

"I'm glad you weren't alone," she said softly.

"Yeah," he said. "Me, too."

They stared at each other for a long moment until a knock at the door forced their gazes apart. Alice popped her head in.

"Good news," she said. "It looks like you'll be discharged by this evening. The doctor will be in to discuss it with you soon."

Bella thanked her then glanced up at Henry and pretended to make a face, desperate to lighten the mood between them, to firmly stow the past back where it belonged. "I thought you said you were going to shower."

He smirked, sniffed under one armpit then the other. "I stink that bad, huh?"

"Worse than that time you burnt the entire batch of minestrone soup." She shook her head in mock-reproof. "It was an eight-quart pot. I don't know how you managed that."

He raised one brow. "I seem to remember one very specific distraction."

Bella's cheeks heated, remembering exactly how good that *distraction* had been. "Get out of here," she ordered.

"I'm going"—he kissed the top of her head—"but I'll be back in a little bit, okay?"

"I'm—"

"Don't say fine." He strode for the door. "I'll be back."

She huffed. "The least you could do is say that in your best Arnold impression."

"You still like the *Terminator* movies?" He paused on the threshold.

"Of course." She rolled her eyes. "They never get old."

"Good," he said. "You and me, *Terminator* marathon at my place tonight."

No, that wasn't going to happen. She was going back to the bed and breakfast and would find a place to stay in the next few days. There would be no crashing at Henry's house. She wasn't a weakling with no other plans or a place to stay.

Bella would find a way to make it work.

On her own.

"I'm—" she called.

The door shut behind him, cutting her off.

And Isabella flopped back in the bed, dizzy from the turn of events. Anger to acceptance. A dash of heat. Decisions that had wrecked everything but hadn't made one lick of difference.

But Henry didn't hate her.

She'd take that.

She still wasn't staying at his house though.

"STOP ARGUING," he growled. "Your brain was *bleeding* yesterday. You're not staying alone at the bed and breakfast."

"I wouldn't be alone," she snapped, batting his hands away when he tried to lift her from the wheelchair the hospital had insisted on pushing her out in. "Anastasia lives there."

He crossed his arms, jaw flexing as she maneuvered herself into his car.

Would it have been easier to let him help her?

Yes.

Less painful?

Probably.

Were those two facts going to change her mind about letting him help?

Hell no.

And . . . *there*. She made it into the seat without falling flat on her face, so that was a win. Bella had to take them where they came because she had the feeling she was going to lose the battle about staying at Henry's house.

He pushed the wheelchair back to the nurse waiting at the hospital's doors. She'd wisely chosen to step away from their argument.

"Your stuff is at my house," Henry said, plunking into the driver's seat and starting up the car. "It makes sense to stay there. At least for tonight."

"Fine."

He'd been shifting into drive, but her agreement had him freezing. "What?"

"It's a rational point," she said.

"I know it is," Henry replied. "Hence, me suggesting it. I just didn't expect you to be—"

"Rational?"

His hands rose in surrender. "You said it, not me."

She snorted.

"I was going to say something to the effect that our arguments never used to resolve themselves this easily."

Bella shrugged. "Maybe we've both matured."

A beat of quiet before they both started laughing.

"Not likely," he said, reaching over and lightly squeezing her hand. "I don't think stubbornness declines with age." He put the car into drive and pulled out of the parking lot.

"Henry?"

His eyes were on the road as he checked for oncoming traffic. "Hmm?"

"I like arguing with you."

He wasn't looking at her, but she still saw his cheek crease as he smiled. "I like arguing with you, too, sweetheart."

And then Bella shut up and let Henry drive her home.

NINE

Henry

HE LIFTED A SLEEPING Isabella out of his car just over twenty minutes later, and Henry realized he could have saved himself an argument if he'd just agreed with Bella about taking her to the B&B and then just driven her around until she fell asleep.

Note to self for next time.

Stifling a chuckle, he carried her through the garage and into the house.

His phone buzzed as he set her on his bed, and he tugged the blanket up and around her before quietly leaving the room. Another vibration came just as he extracted his cell from his pocket.

Henry glanced at the screen and saw that it was a message from Rob. And Kelly.

"Shit," he muttered, knowing that word had gotten out and it was only a matter of time before his friends descended on his house to get a glimpse of Isabella.

Thus, he dealt with Rob first. It was easier, a request that

Henry bring Bella to the station the following morning. He sent a reply, telling Rob that he'd text when she was up the next day.

Kelly was more problematic.

She didn't know anything that had happened in New York.

And if she found out that Bella had hurt him so deeply, his best friend's protectiveness would most definitely come out.

But then he read her text.

I already like her because you like her, just remember that before you try to push me away. I love you.

Well, didn't he feel like an asshole?

It's not that, Kel.

Lies.

I've known you since kindergarten. Don't try that B.S. with me.

Of course, she'd called him on it. He'd always had a fondness for strong women—Kelly, Bella, Melissa, his mother—and had been lucky enough to have plenty of them in his life. But in this moment, after battling with Bella, with Kel holding his feet to the fire, he thought he might see the appeal of a doormat.

He snorted, walking down the hall to the kitchen.

Okay, that was another lie.

There was something about a woman with fire inside her that was utterly entrancing. No, it didn't always make things easy nor did it make for smooth sailing, but he wouldn't trade Bella for a limp dish towel.

After grabbing a beer from the fridge, he crossed over to his couch and flicked on the TV, pondering what to say to Kel.

Eventually, he decided on the truth.

She's the one from NYC, Kel. I need time to figure it out.

A heartbeat later and she'd confirmed why she was his best friend.

I figured. Just know I'm here when you come out the other side. Or if you need a midnight vent session. God knows the twins get me up often enough ;)

He popped the top on his beer.

I love you.

His phone vibrated.

That's because I'm extremely loveable.

Henry shook his head, but he was smiling. He'd gotten lucky in kindergarten when he'd punched that little asshole who'd been tormenting Kelly. It was an auspicious start to a friendship, but one he couldn't regret.

Of course, he was also *really* lucky she'd turned him down when he'd proposed.

He picked up the remote and scrolled through the channels. There was a Gold Hockey game on—not the closest team, but one of the local kids had been drafted by them a few years back, and Henry always got a kick out of watching Blue on the ice.

The kid had moves.

During second intermission, the hairs on the back of his neck prickled. He glanced over his shoulder and saw Bella hobbling down the hall.

May the hockey gods give him patience because Henry was damn sure that the doctor who'd discharged her had made Bella promise to take it easy on that leg.

He pushed to his feet, ready to remind her of exactly that, when she stumbled.

Two quick steps and he was there, catching her arm and helping her over to the couch.

"Thanks," she murmured.

He grunted, grabbed her bottle of pain pills off the table and handed her one, along with a bottle of water he'd snagged from the kitchen.

Bella didn't argue with him, and that told Henry enough about her condition. She was hurting, and he needed to give her space, no matter the tempting picture she made sprawled out on his couch.

Her lips curved into a tremulous smile after she'd handed him back the bottle. "I didn't realize you had such a long hall."

He snorted, his own lips turning up. "Either that or you're stubborn to a fault?"

She shrugged—or attempted to anyway, aborting the motion mid-move with a wince. "We've established that fact already." Her nose wrinkled before he could confirm or deny that particular statement . . . which was probably a good thing. "I need to get out of these clothes."

Henry's gaze drifted down. She was wearing a pair of donated pale blue scrubs, since he hadn't thought to bring her a change of clothes. Not that he was complaining—the set was slightly too small, emphasizing the curve of her breasts and hips, dipping low on the front.

Yes, he knew she was convalescing.

No, he wasn't dead.

Isabella was beautiful, and sex had never been their problem. Since he'd begun acknowledging his own role in the events from five years before, his brain was having a hell of a time reminding his body that she'd given him absolutely no reason to think that she might still be attracted to him.

Also, this just in, he was an asshole to be popping a boner when she was injured.

What was he? Sixteen and hormone ridden?

Henry was a grown man, and he shouldn't be studying that exposed V of skin between her breasts like it was an oasis and he was a parched man in the desert.

But good intentions or not, he *had* noticed that sliver of skin. And he couldn't *un*-notice it.

Not as she shifted to lie sideways on the couch so the cushions supported her hip. Not as he helped her. Not as the too-tight top slid up and his hand accidentally brushed the soft skin on her side.

He jerked it back, but it was too late. The shock of awareness had hit him like a ton of bricks.

Bella's breath hitched, eyes flashing wide.

"That—"

Henry straightened. "I'll go grab you some food. I'm sure you're still hungry."

White teeth nibbled on a pink bottom lip. He wanted it to be *his* teeth, *his* mouth.

Not the right time. Too soon. Too—

"Henry?"

He blinked, focused back on the woman in front of him, instead of the swirling mass of thoughts in his mind. "Yeah?"

"Will you touch me again?"

TEN

Bella

DAMN.

She'd broken him.

Bella had asked him to touch her and in response, he was rooted in place, jaw clenched, shoulders stiff.

"Henry?" she prodded.

That got him moving . . . or at least blinking. And after a moment, he glanced over at her, eyes tracing down over her body and jaw tightening further.

Because he wanted to touch her? Or—worse—because he didn't?

"You're probably hungry," he said, angling his body away from hers.

Because he didn't want her.

Damn.

She couldn't lie. That hurt. Here she was drooling over the man, admiring the way he'd filled out over the last few years. He'd gotten harder, muscles more defined, thicker in all the right places, not to mention the scruff on his jaw he was sporting. She wanted that rubbing in *all* sorts of places.

Her throat, her breasts, between her thighs—

But he didn't want that. He'd forgiven her, and that alone was enough.

"Yeah," she agreed. "Food would be great."

So would an orgasm, but Bella was trying to be grateful for what she had. She was safe, Henry was there, and even though she'd woken to images of Sergio's hands were wrapped around her throat again—

"What is it?" A finger brushed the back of her hand, and she opened her eyes to see Henry had come close.

He was touching her, though not in the way she really wanted.

Greedy mofo, wasn't she?

She forced a smile. "I'm—"

One fingertip pressed to her lips, stalling the rest of her statement. "You finish that sentence, and I'll forget my intentions to leave you alone to heal."

"Why would I need to be left alone?" He didn't move his hand when she replied, and the sensation of that roughened finger skimming over her lips as they moved sent shivers down her spine.

"Because you're hurting."

"Not so much anymore."

He slid his hand lower, the back skimming along her throat, fluttering over one collarbone then the other. "Then why do your eyes look like that?"

Bella frowned. "Like what?"

"Shadowed."

Her lungs froze. "I'm just tired is all."

"Nope. That's not it."

Ugh. There were two reasons, dammit, that her eyes were quote-unquote *shadowed,* and she didn't want to share either of them with Henry. "Do you have anything you can heat up for me?" she asked, instead of divulging the truth. "I really am quite hungry."

One brown brow lifted.

Waiting for an answer.

In the end, she told him the lesser of two evils because she'd rather be viewed as horny than a pathetic coward who'd fled the bedroom at the first sign of a nightmare.

"Fine." She huffed. "I want you, okay? You're sexy and gorgeous and my pussy has been very lonely as of late—" She clamped one hand to her mouth, closed her eyes.

The damned pain pill was loosening her tongue because she had *not* just said that.

"You and Sergio didn't—"

The name made her flinch and quickly shake her head.

Bella reveled in the feeling for a moment, the swish-swish of her brain floating in her skull. She almost would have thought she was drunk, except no booze.

Just very strong pain pills apparently.

Well, note to future self, no more of those.

"No," she said. "Sergio and I did. At first. Just lately, I couldn't—"

This was wrong. Telling Henry about her bedroom life with Sergio.

"Couldn't what?"

She dropped her head back to the arm of the couch. "It doesn't matter."

He sank onto the cushion near her feet, plunking them into his lap and rubbing the arches. "It matters to me."

"He couldn't make me come, okay?" She sighed. "No one can, except for you and my vibrator"—her lips pursed—"and only one of those is always at the ready."

"First, know that I'll be circling back to the orgasm thing in a moment because I'm *always* ready when you're around." Henry shifted his hips, and her foot bumped against—*oh*, she liked *that* a whole hell of a lot. "But more importantly, why don't you think I want you?"

"Because I hurt you. Because you don't want to touch me and maybe things will never be the same between us again. Because you got all pretty and handsome, and *my* boobs are saggy, and I've got cellulite and—" She squealed when Henry reached for the hem of her top. "What are you doing?"

"Seeing what's sagged."

She slapped his hands away. "Not a chance, Henry Miller."

He chuckled. "There's my girl." A squeeze to her feet. "I'm going to say this once, so pay attention."

Bella raised one finger. "Just so you're aware, I think that pill has gone to my head." Her voice dropped to a whisper. "I think I'm high."

"Focus," Henry said, though he was smiling. "I guess I'll be open to saying it twice, in case my lightweight of a woman doesn't hear it the first time—"

"Hey."

"I gave you a quarter of a pill."

"So?"

"So *nothing*," he said before his eyes went serious enough that any more words stalled in her throat. "You're beautiful. End of story. I want you even though you're hurting and slightly high. I've wanted you from the moment that I first saw you in Brian's kitchen." He reached up to cup her cheek. "Wanting isn't the issue."

Her heart skipped a beat. "Then what is?"

"It's been five years."

Her brows pulled down. "Yeah, so?"

"You were just engaged to a bastard that hurt you."

"S-Sergio doesn't matter."

Henry sighed. "Except he does. Because he's the reason for the shadows. Maybe you *are* worried that things between us won't be the same if we try to see where things go." A shrug. "But that's not all of it. And you know what? I hope it's *not* the same between us. I hope we've grown up a little because I want things between us to end differently."

She sucked in a breath.

"In fact"—his eyes warmed—"I don't know that I want them to end at all."

"Henry—"

"I know." He sat up. "I know it's crazy and too soon, and while I definitely want to take things slow between us, I also know that I've never felt one iota for another woman what I feel for you. You've always meant *so* much, sweetheart, and I want to see where things go—"

"I'm high."

He smirked. "Yes, I know."

"No," she said. "I must be really, crazy high because you did not just say those things, Henry. You did *not* just give me hope. You *didn't*—"

"I'm right there with you, baby. Big feelings, big risk, big hope."

"But I hurt you," she whispered.

"You weren't ready, and I pushed." He shrugged. "I wish you hadn't left, that you'd stuck around and explained your feelings, but we can't go back now."

Oh, God. She had to tell him why she'd left. She understood now. It wasn't shameful. She'd sacrificed everything for the man she loved, and Henry had to know that.

He had to know he meant *that* much.

"I—"

"I want to forget about the past. I want you to stay, and we can see if we're as compatible now as we were back then."

"I want that, too, but—"

He kissed her.

She was dizzy from the pain pill, from her emotions, from the heavy weight of the past, but the feel of Henry's lips against hers made all of that disappear.

Heat was the first thing to take over. It began at her mouth, spreading down and outward, making the tips of her fingers tingle, her breasts swell and ache, her stomach flutter, and her thighs press tightly together, an ache of an altogether different kind filling the space in between.

She wanted him on top of her. Inside her—

Bella gasped when his tongue slid into her mouth, tangling with hers. He'd moved so he was alongside her, his back to the cushions and his deliciously hard chest against her side. Fingers wove into her hair, coaxing her head back, as he brought their mouths more firmly together.

Oh, God.

He kept his hands in her hair and though she wanted them to move lower, to tease and soothe all her various aches, she knew he was taking it slow.

Well, if a heart-shatteringly, hot as fuck kiss that had almost reduced her to ashes could be considered *slow*.

Regardless, aside from their bodies touching lengthwise, Henry's hands were decidedly less busy than his mouth. But that didn't mean *hers* had to be. She rested them on his chest, squeezing the yummy pair of pecs she found there for a moment before sliding lower.

Henry broke away, hot puffs of air teasing her lips.

Bella tilted her head, wanting his mouth again, but he carefully extracted himself and sat up.

"I think I promised you food."

She propped herself up on her elbows, trying desperately to clear her spinning mind as he slid from behind her and found his feet. "Henry—"

"Dangerous." He pressed a kiss to her forehead. "Beautiful woman." One more kiss before he turned and headed into the kitchen, the sound of pots and pans and cheerful whistling drifting into the living room.

When he returned a few minutes later, two plates in hand, and Bella saw what he'd made her, her heart swelled with hope all over again.

Maybe this time they would be different.

Because he'd made her a Cobb salad.

ELEVEN

Henry

HE WAS COOKING for the breakfast rush.

He definitely didn't want to be, but Frank had caught a cold, Michelle, his other full-timer, was working the evening shift, and Steven, the part-time chef he was training, was away on a trip with his girlfriend that they'd both been saving up for. Henry wasn't about to ruin that.

Bella had fallen asleep over salads, and so he'd carried her into the bedroom, tucking her safely under the blankets, knowing that her body needed all the rest it could get.

He'd slept in the spare bedroom and had woken to the smell of freshly brewed coffee.

Yeah, he could get used to that. Not the sleeping alone on the cramped twin bed part, but the waking up to find a beautiful woman in his house.

He especially could get used to the sight of Bella in his kitchen. She'd thrown together a crepe batter, sliced berries, and freshly whipped cream.

All before five in the morning.

The sun hadn't been up, the call to his cell had woken him for a shift that wasn't normally his, and so he could have still been sleeping—and he was old enough to really appreciate his sleep—but Henry hadn't been able to summon up one fuck to give.

Not when he was able to watch Bella cook crepes for a few minutes, her hips swaying slightly from side to side as she hummed a soft song.

Obviously, she felt better, and the delicious breakfast she'd made had been a nice by-product, but Henry hadn't been able to shake the rightness of the moment.

Bella was right.

And he could still taste her on his tongue, even though it had been hours since he'd dropped her off at the police station, even though he'd tasted a plethora of other dishes since eating her crepes—

He smirked as he imagined Kel chiming in with a comment along the lines of *"So that's what the kids are calling it nowadays?"*

So wrong.

And yet so right because he'd like to eat Bella's—

"Fuck." Henry hissed out a pained breath and whipped his hand back. He'd burnt himself because he was spending too much time focusing on Bella's *crepes* and not enough time on the growing pile of tickets in front of him. "Shit," he muttered, grabbing the pan off the heat and sticking his hand under a stream of cold water for a few precious seconds.

It was enough to take the edge off the pain and to reduce the burn to a dull throb.

Henry had burned himself often enough to know that the injury would kindly remind him of its presence throughout the day, but he didn't have any more time to waste.

The thing about breakfast was that it had to be made fast

and served even faster. No one wanted to eat cold eggs or bacon or pancakes. Of course, that meant he had to have way too many pans working at the same time and that he definitely didn't have time to be slowed down by a burn.

He dried his hands on a towel and slid the pan back onto the burner, keeping his head down and his mind focused on cooking until he'd dug himself out of the hole he'd made, a good half hour later.

Sweat soaked through his T-shirt, and the front of his apron was splattered with grease and pancake batter and—

"You used to cook a lot more cleanly."

He'd be lying if he'd said his heart hadn't skipped a beat when he looked up and saw Bella leaning against the door, a smile teasing the corners of her mouth.

Her eyes were brighter today, her shoulders more relaxed.

Even the bruising and abrasions on her face were beginning to fade.

"I learned from the best," he said, stepping away from the stove and checking for any new tickets. Figuring that he had at least a couple minutes, Henry stripped off his apron and hung it on a peg then took Bella's hand and led her down the hall to his office.

She scoffed but followed him. "My workstation was always clean."

"Is that what you call being doused in flour?"

Her eyes narrowed. "That was one time, and you know it was because the bag had a tear in it."

"If you say so," he teased.

She growled, trying to extricate her hand from his, but they'd reached his office, so he just tugged her over the threshold, shut the door behind them, and lowered his head to hers.

Her hands came up to his shoulders and he half-expected

her to push him away, but then they slid around the back of his neck and pulled him closer.

So. Fucking. Good.

Her tongue danced with his, darting in and out in a rhythm they'd perfected five years before and they stayed like that, kissing until his lungs screamed for air. Henry drew back, but he needed to keep touching her. He slid his hands up and down her sides, bent to nip at her jaw, her throat.

"Henry," she moaned and one leg wrapped around his waist.

He barely had a brain cell left to register the blip that came with his woman potentially hurting herself from the action, but then she tilted her pelvis, aligning it firmly against his cock and groaning in pleasure.

The single cell poofed away like so much smoke.

He lifted her, pressing her spine to the door and took her mouth in another head-spinning kiss.

It was glorious. It was absolute heaven.

Until the knock at the door.

"Henry?" came Rachelle's voice. She was one of the two waitresses on the schedule that morning.

He cleared his throat, cock aching, chest heaving. "Yeah?"

"We've got a bunch of tickets piling up."

Bella slid one leg to the floor then the other, and the loss of feeling her pressed so intimately against him was almost enough to make Henry cry.

"Just changing my shirt," he called. "Be out in two minutes."

"Roger that," Rachelle said. "Did Isabella find you?"

Yes, the whole town now knew Isabella by name, and their protectiveness for him had morphed into sympathy and protectiveness for her. All of that was thanks to Esther's social media prowess.

He wanted to be her when he grew up.

Though, maybe minus the ogling.

"Not yet," he lied.

"Hmm. I'll go look for her, tell her you were changing, and that you'll be back in the kitchen in a minute."

"Thanks," he said.

Bella giggled as they listened to the sound of Rachelle's footsteps moving back down the hall.

"Hush you," he said, making sure she was steady before whipping around to find a clean T-shirt. He tugged off his sweaty one and tossed it to the side, then turned in a rush when he heard her make a noise that sounded like choking. "You oka—"

"Oh, thank you, Jesus," she murmured, eyes on his chest, his stomach, lower.

"Bella, sweetheart, you can't look at me like that," he groaned.

She licked her lips.

And fuck, but his cock threatened to break in half.

"Put on the damn shirt," she hissed, slamming her eyes closed and turning to scrabble for the door handle.

Her actions weren't in the correct order, obviously, and so she was still fumbling around by the time Henry shrugged on the shirt and crossed back over to her. "It's safe to look now," he said, brushing her hands away and turning the knob. "Come on. You can keep me company in the kitchen."

Better than him stripping her naked in his office or burning the entire restaurant down, he realized with a sigh as they slipped back into the kitchen, because he'd forgotten to turn a burner off. Luckily, it was his practice to keep everything except for the actual food cooking away from the open flames, and them staying on for hours on end *wasn't* unusual. Since nothing was cooking at the moment, everything was good.

But still, he didn't typically leave the flames unattended.

He'd been too cautious to risk it after his father had started a grease fire.

The right practice, he'd decided long ago, was to shut everything off if it was going to be unattended, even for a few minutes.

Apparently, the cautious part of his brain had left the building when Bella had shown up in his kitchen.

Be smart, H-man. But don't forget to live.

Hearing his father's voice, even just in his mind, was like a punch directly to the gut. The words were one of his favorite sayings.

Don't forget to live.

Well, Henry certainly felt alive for the first time in years.

Bella tugged her hand from his then walked over and grabbed two clean aprons, dropping one over her head before handing him the other. She clapped her hands together. "All right, chef. Where do we start?"

"No, sweetheart." He pointed to the stool. "You should rest."

She rolled her eyes. "I'll just remind you before that pile of tickets gets any bigger that your orders don't work on me and that all arguments end in my favor."

"Not all—" he began then broke off with a sigh when she raised a brow.

Okay, fine, even if it wasn't *all* of them, Henry definitely didn't have time for an argument in *this* instance.

He thought fast, picking up tickets and scanning them, trying to find an item that wouldn't tax her too much.

"Can you do pancakes?" he asked.

Pancakes were a safe bet, especially with breakfast winding down and the batter already made.

She scoffed. "With one arm tied behind my back."

Henry scooped up a stool and placed it in front of the griddle. "How about with a chair under your bottom instead?"

Bella rolled her eyes, but she didn't argue about that, so Henry considered it a win.

"Ready?" he asked, going back to the tickets and picking up the first one.

"Yes, chef."

His lips twitched at her pert response before his amusement faded and he began calling out items.

The next couple of hours passed in a flash.

Breakfast turned to lunch and pancakes became grilled cheese and patty melts, and Henry couldn't remember a time he'd had as much fun in the kitchen as he was having that day. Bella was tart and endearing in equal terms, and she was scarily efficient, having familiarized herself with the kitchen in record time.

When he'd questioned her about it, she'd shrugged and said it was like the restaurants they'd worked at while in New York.

Henry supposed that was true.

He'd reorganized after his father died. Aside from everything needing a deep clean, Henry hadn't been able to work in the cluttered space. He hadn't had the brainpower or energy to come up with his own system, and so he'd transplanted one that he knew like the back of his hand.

The diner's kitchen was pristine. It was organized. And it was filled to the brim with Bella.

Henry decided he liked it that way.

She wiped her forehead on a towel after they finished the final lunch rush ticket, and he wanted to kiss her all over again.

But he didn't.

Because when he kissed this women, his mind went to mush, and Michelle was due in at any moment. But then Bella smiled up at him, a few strands of deep brown hair having slid free of her ponytail to curl around her face. She was incredible and . . . he forgot about being good.

He needed to live.

Henry pressed his mouth to hers the exact moment Michelle strode into the kitchen, bellowing, "The savior is here! Oh gross! Stop sucking face. That's not sanitary."

Bella jumped back from him, eyes widening.

"Get on tickets, Michelle," he told his employee. "All the prep is done for tonight."

"Wow, you can kiss *and* cook?" She raised a brow.

He glared. "You're fired."

Bella gasped, but Michelle just grinned. "He's kidding," she told Bella. "Henry fires me at least once a week."

"Unfortunately, she does *not* stay fired," he grumbled.

Bella's lips twitched. He slipped off his apron, helped her out of hers. "Call me if you need anything."

"I won't."

He sighed. "Humor me."

Michelle sighed. "Okay, I promise if I get into an existential food crisis, I will call you because I do *not* need help with dinner service." She pointed to the door. "Now go forth and kissy face. I've got the diner."

They exchanged goodbyes and waves before heading out into the hall.

"Now what?" Bella asked as they stopped long enough in his office for him to retrieve his wallet and car keys.

He thought about that for a long moment.

"Everything good at the station?"

She hesitated for the briefest moment before nodding. That short delay had Henry making a mental note to confirm things with Rob later. But for now, he wanted to spend some time with Bella outside of the kitchen.

"Want to see something cool?"

TWELVE

Bella

HER BREATH CAUGHT as she stepped out of Henry's car.

Rolling hills of green for as far as the eye could see. The wide-open space was dotted with the occasional tree, but the real show-stealer was the sky. It was absolutely beautiful in shades of orange and red and blue.

How did it seem larger than life here in Utah? It wasn't as if she'd never looked up at the sky before.

Was it Henry?

Or maybe it was the fact that she was finally making some decisions for herself.

She'd left. Her father wouldn't control her any longer.

And she had Henry . . . or at least a potential with him.

So, dammit, she was allowed to feel a little buoyant and hopeful and—

Fingers brushed the space between her eyebrows. "What's got you looking so fierce?"

She turned to him. "I was thinking that I've stared up at the sky my entire life and that I've never seen it look so beautiful.

Also," she added before he could reply. "I was thinking how lucky I was to have a second chance with you and vowing not to screw it up."

He snorted. "*I'm* the lucky one."

"No, I'm—" Bella stopped, smirking up at him. "Is this our version of I-love-you more/No-I-love-*you*-more?"

"God, I hope not." He slipped an arm around her waist, pausing when she stiffened in surprise to ask, "This okay?"

She hurried to nod. "It's"—her teeth found her lip, bit down —"actually really nice."

"Actually nice?"

"Don't push it." She glared.

"Come on," he said with a chuckle. "This isn't what I wanted to show you. Or not all of it anyway." He led her over the crest of a hill, and she gaped at the huge boulder perched on the opposite side. "It's silly, but this has been my place since I was little."

Bella let him help her up on top of the giant rock. It was taller than her, but a series of foot and hand holds made it easy enough to scale. Her hip gave only the slightest protest as she pulled herself on top.

"Wow," she murmured.

The view was even prettier from there. A river snaked through a valley in the distance, spreading a deep emerald green along its length.

He pointed to the right. "That's Roosevelt Ranch over there."

Squinting, she could make out a few buildings tucked into the landscape. "Ah, the home of my aborted wedding," she said with a sigh. "It looks as gorgeous as the pictures made it seem. Is it true that the stables are as big as the house?"

"Since Kel enlarged them, yes." He tucked back a strand of

hair that had come loose from her ponytail. "How did Sergio know about Roosevelt Ranch?"

"He caught me looking up Darlington." She wrinkled her nose. "I know I shouldn't say caught because it implies I was doing something wrong. The truth was that I kept tabs on you over the years. The diner's Yelp page is bookmarked on my laptop."

"What?"

"Pathetic, I know. I'd vowed I'd stop when I got married, but I'd wanted to make sure you were okay, and that meant I spent a lot of time searching for news articles about you or Darlington."

"Bella—"

"Talk about silly," she said with a laugh, words coming faster because the fact that she'd cyber-stalked her ex was critically embarrassing. "But I knew about Roosevelt Ranch because it came up in the news a lot for its breeding program." She shrugged. "I used to pretend that I was here instead of there"—and she was venturing into dangerous territory—"so this view living up to expectations is amazing."

"Sweetheart—"

"I also heard about murderous deer and a drug ring that involved a corrupt FBI agent, but that was more of a national story—"

His finger pressed to her lips, cutting off the flow of words.

One large hand plunked onto her thigh, squeezed gently. "There's a lot to unpack there. Hold tight," he added when she opened her mouth to reply. "Because I think what's most important is for me to know why you wanted to be here instead of there." He bent so his eyes were level with hers. "Sweetheart, if you wanted to come, why did you wait for years?"

That was the question of the hour.

Her gaze flitted to the hills. "It's complicated."

"I've got time for complicated."

Bella wavered for a moment more. If she told him the truth, would it make things better or worse? She didn't want him to feel bad that she'd done what she'd done, but at the same time, she needed him to know that she'd loved him enough to sacrifice for him.

And in the end, *that* was what decided it for her.

Henry mattered. He needed to know that.

"We met in New York."

He nodded. "Yeah, that's right."

"We fell in love there, we cooked and lived together and were building a future with each other."

"Yes." It was more cautious now.

"But I was lying to you then. Not about us," she rushed to say. "Just about my life back home. I made it seem like my family supported my decision to move away and go to culinary school." She shook her head. "The truth is that they were adamantly against it, and it was only because my mother left me a small trust fund after she passed that I was able to go.

"My father controlled *everything*. What my mother and I wore, what we ate, what I studied at university." Bella blew out a breath, remembering the misery of those years. Things had gotten slightly easier when her mother had fallen ill because they hadn't been trotted out to functions every night of the week like prized bulls. But then her mother had died, and things had gotten exponentially harder.

"I didn't know," he said.

Bella smiled, though she knew it was sad. "No one did. I was really good at pretending. But obviously, my mother knew what he was like, and she made sure the money she left me was in my name only."

On her death bed, she'd forced Isabella to promise her that she would go after her dream.

It was what had given her the courage to go to culinary school in the first place.

And pay for it all up front, in case her father found a way to wrest away control of that money.

She hadn't considered failing or not liking it, not for a moment.

That had been her chance to get out.

"My father thought it was just me sowing my wild oats, that I would run out of money and come home, but he underestimated me."

Henry smiled and cupped her cheek. "What did you do?"

"I graduated, got a job in New York. A shitty one at first and a shitty apartment to go with it. But it was mine, and I was finally *living*. It was fabulous."

"I used to love watching you in the restaurant," he murmured. "You'd take such joy in the process."

She sighed, resting her head on his shoulder. "I did love it."

"So then what happened?"

"I met you. We fell in love." She hesitated. "And your dad got sick."

He stiffened.

"It's not like you think," she whispered. "I remember all the phone calls, how upset you were when things weren't looking good. I-I overheard you and your mom talking about how you couldn't afford the surgery."

She straightened, studying his face, but Bella couldn't read anything in his expression. It was blank, his eyes guarded.

"I didn't have enough left," she murmured. "My money had gone to school, to living costs when I initially moved to New York. And my father had been pressuring me to come home for a long time. He wanted me to get married—"

Henry's eyes went dark. "To Sergio?"

"No," she said. "Not him, at first. He had someone else picked out."

His expression hardened, and her heart skipped a beat. Every cowardly inch of her was saying to stop here, that Henry didn't need to know everything. But . . .

He *did* need to know.

"I told him, no, obviously. I was with you, and I thought— well, I thought you and I would eventually get married," she said, watching as his lungs expanded as he took a deep breath. "But then your dad got worse, and you were leaving, and the surgery was his last hope . . ."

"No. *No.*" Henry shot to his feet, and the speed of it startled her, almost toppling her from the boulder. He steadied her then jumped down to the ground, thrusting a hand through his hair as he paced.

After a long minute, he turned back to her.

"Bella, sweetheart, tell me you *didn't*. Tell me you didn't leave so my dad—"

He broke off, pain in his eyes, his words.

She swallowed. "I had to."

"Fuck." He spun away. "*Fuck.* All this time I thought—" He turned, walking back toward her, head in his hands.

She shifted, wanting to get off the boulder, to go to him, but froze when he clambered back up the rock and stopped, his face only inches from hers. "Why, baby? Why would you do that?"

"It was the only way for your dad to have the surgery . . ."

His eyes closed and for a moment, Bella thought he'd stopped breathing, but then he was crushing her to him, his arms wrapping tightly around her, his breaths in shaky exhales.

"Y-you shouldn't have done that. You shouldn't have. You shouldn't—"

She hugged him back. "I had to."

"No."

"Yes."

He leaned back, eyes slightly reddened. "*No.*"

She crossed her arms. "Yes."

Henry sighed. "At the very least, you should have told me."

"And you would have let me do it?" She raised one brow.

"Of course not."

Bella huffed. "Well, that's exactly why I *had* to."

"You had to unilaterally decide the future of our relationship?"

Oh, he was mad.

Well, tough shit.

Because she was mad, too.

She popped to her feet—not a smart thing to do when perched atop a boulder. Henry caught her before she toppled down the hill, gripping the tops of her arms and looking as though he wanted to shake some sense into her.

Hmph.

She wanted to shake some sense into *him.*

"It was the only thing I could do," she snapped. "*I* had the opportunity to help your father get the surgery, and—"

"It didn't make one bit of difference in the end!" He clenched his jaw. "All it meant was that I lost him *and* you."

Her breath caught. "I know."

But she wasn't going to apologize for doing it. If she hadn't gone, if she hadn't gotten the money and figured out a way to get Henry's dad the surgery, she wouldn't have been able to live with herself knowing that she hadn't done everything in her power to help him.

She might not have ever met Henry's dad, but Henry was engrained in her heart and though she didn't want to hurt him, she would do it all again in the end, if it meant that his dad had been given every chance to live. Broken hearts could heal, or at least the *emotionally* shattered ones could. The physically malfunctioning ones needed outside help.

She'd done that and as much as she'd hated to be without him in her life for that many years, as painful and wrenching as it had been, it was what she'd *had* to do.

"I can see it in your face," he grumbled. "I can see that no matter what I say, it won't change your mind that you did the right thing."

"That's because I did."

He shook his head. "*Woman*," he warned.

"*Man*," she countered.

His lips curved, hers followed suit.

She touched his cheek. "You're not mad anymore?"

"I'm furious." He picked up her hand, pressed a kiss to her palm. "But I understand why you did it."

Bella let out a relieved breath.

He tugged them both back down to sitting, tucked her firmly against his side. "Why didn't you come back sooner?"

"I only just found out your dad died."

Clarity danced across his eyes. "The newspaper article about the diner."

"Yes." She'd been doing her weekly search of Darlington news, living vicariously in her mind, pretending that she was part of the mix—maybe she'd take horseback riding lessons at the ranch, open a little bakery downtown—when she'd spied the article about Henry honoring the five-year anniversary of his father's death by serving his favorite dishes for half off, with all proceeds going to a heart health charity.

She'd seen Henry's picture in the article. He'd been smiling down at Kelly Roosevelt as she'd held a tray filled with plates on her shoulder.

He'd looked so happy.

And she'd known that she couldn't marry Sergio.

Even if Henry never forgave her, even if they never had a future together, she couldn't tie herself to a man who didn't make her feel the same things that Henry did.

She hadn't even planned on coming to Utah in the first place. But after she'd slipped out of her father's estate and made it to the airport, she'd discovered that the first international flight had been to Salt Lake City.

Kismet.

That was the only explanation.

Now she was here, and Henry knew everything, but he was still staring down at her with affection in his eyes.

"You're so beautiful," he said.

Her heart skipped a beat. When he said those things like that, like he believed them, she felt so damned much. "I've missed you."

He tucked her head back onto his shoulder, kissed the top of her head. "I'm just glad you're here now."

"Me, too," she murmured.

They sat like that, watching the sun sink lower in the sky, the reds and oranges of earlier transforming into navy and black. Only when the stars had started to peek out at them did Henry slip from the boulder and help her down.

Her hip protested after sitting so long in one position, but it quickly loosened up as they hiked back up the hill then down the other side.

"So," he said, pulling open her door, "does this mean you're going to be my girlfriend?"

She smiled. "You've got to date me first."

"You're living in my house. I think that constitutes as dating."

"I won't be living there for long. Pam told me about an apartment above the bookstore downtown. She gave me the landlord's number today."

He was frowning down at her, so she tugged the door closed, cutting off whatever argument he was going to throw her way. "Why would you do that?" he asked, plopping down into his seat. "We lived together in New York. We—"

Bella dropped her hand to his thigh. "I need this time to work on me."

A snort. "That's a brush-off line if I ever heard one."

"I need to figure out who I am without Sergio, without my father pulling the strings."

He made a face.

"Also, I love you," she said. "I've never stopped, but that doesn't mean we shouldn't take things slow. For God's sake, I've only been in town three days and we're already playing house."

"I—" He shook his head. "You still love me?"

Bella patted his cheek. "Don't be stupid."

"I—"

"Am going to give me time."

Henry sighed. "I love you."

"You'll let me lease the apartment?"

One brow came up. "Considering I own it? Yes, you can stay in it for as long as you want."

She'd guessed as much when Pam had suggested it with a twinkle in her eyes and a smirk on her lips. "And you'll charge me rent?"

He shook his head. "If you'll be the diner's pastry chef?"

"Does a diner *need* a pastry chef?"

"*I* need you and believe me, the customers will kill for your food. Hell, most of the pies and cakes are your recipes anyway."

"Fine," she said. "I'll work for you until I save up enough money to open my bakery." A shrug. "God knows, I need the practice. Today was my first time in the kitchen in five years."

"What a waste." He touched her cheek. "A bakery?"

"Yeah. I've always wanted to own one."

He kissed her. One press of his lips and her head was spinning, desire swimming through her body, urging her to crawl over the console and into his lap. But before she could do that, he broke away, hot breath fanning over her lips.

Calloused fingers on her cheek, her throat. "I can't wait to see what you do." Another hot kiss that sent her temperature sky high. "I know it's going to be great."

And damn, if she didn't already love the man, those words would have done it.

"Come on," she said, wrapping her hand around his. "Let's go home."

"Will you promise to feed me?" He waggled his brows.

She laughed. "I thought *you* were the fancy chef?"

"Not anymore," he said, way too innocent as he turned on the ignition and maneuvered the car back down the road. "I'm just a small-town cook." A beat. "Who's really, really hungry."

This man. God, she loved him.

"You just want me to make pasta."

Guilty eyes flicked to hers then back to the road.

Bella stretched over the console to kiss him on the cheek. "How does fettuccini sound?"

"As perfect as you are."

She made a barfing sound, but secretly, Bella loved the sweet words.

THIRTEEN

Henry

HE STARED at the angry woman glaring at him through the window of his front door and sighed.

Really, it had only been a matter of time before this happened.

Bella had been in town for just over two weeks, and he'd spent nearly every waking minute with her. The town was in a whirlwind between her sudden appearance, the incident with Sergio—who'd been released on bail then had promptly skipped town like the bastard he was—and the fact that Henry had spent the last fourteen plus days walking around with a stupid ass grin on his face.

They were also in a frenzy over her baked goods.

He couldn't keep tiramisu in stock, her lemon cream pie had been chosen decisively over his, and her blueberry cobbler had sold out within the first hour.

Three different people had begged Bella to make pans for their birthdays.

And one of their birthdays wasn't for six months.

She'd blushed at the attention, thanking them and promising to make a fresh batch for the following day.

So, yeah, Henry didn't think that Bella's dream of a bakery was that far off.

But *Bella* wasn't the one staring angrily at him as he strode down the hall to his front door.

Nope. Unfortunately for him, that was his mother.

He paused, considering the wrath he'd face if he turned around now and pretended he hadn't seen her.

"Don't you dare!" Her voice was shrill enough to pierce right through the wood and glass.

Girding his loins, he opened the front door.

His mother swept inside, pausing briefly to kiss him on the cheek. "I have been hearing about this blueberry cobbler all week," she said, striding into his kitchen. "It's all the ladies at the Garden Center can talk about, but does my own son bring me any?" A long-suffering sigh. "No. I waited and waited—"

"Mom, you've been home all of one day," he interrupted, sliding past her to open up his fridge. He did, in fact, have a pan of blueberry cobbler hidden away. It had been Bella's *practice run* and though she'd proclaimed it unworthy for sale, he'd thought it was delicious and wouldn't let her throw it away. "Hold the tirade for a minute."

Now, he served up a scoop on a plate and popped it in the microwave.

Bella would have his hide for that later, for daring to put her masterpiece in something as terrible as a microwave, but she'd just have to deal. He needed to get cobbler into his mother's mouth as quickly as possible.

"Up," he told her, pointing to a barstool as the microwave dinged.

Turning, he grabbed a carton of vanilla ice cream from the freezer, spooned some on top, and then passed the plate over.

She all but snatched it from his hands.

Henry waited as she ate, well familiar with her tactics. His mom was sneaky— distract, avert, wait for her opponent's guard to drop . . . then *bam*, a shot directly to the head.

Or maybe, in this case, the heart.

Luckily for him and his budding relationship with Bella, his mother had left the morning Bella had arrived in town. She'd gone on a cruise with some of her girlfriends, returning just the day before.

Which was the only reason he hadn't gotten a visit along these lines before now.

"That is delicious," she said, scraping the side of her spoon across the plate to get every last drop.

"Yes, it is."

"And this Isabella made it?"

He nodded.

"This is the same woman who broke your heart in New York."

Henry took the plate and set it in the sink. "There was a misunderstanding."

"Hmm." She sat back, crossed her arms. "Has Kelly met her?"

"Not yet." He mirrored her position. "The kids are keeping her busy."

"And also because you told her to stay away."

He could almost hear the arrow swooshing through the air, the *thunk* as it struck a bull's-eye. Also, Kelly was a big, fat traitor for telling his mother that fact.

"She's worried about you."

Well, now that was a lie. Kel hadn't swooped in like his mom, but she *had* been texting him and the theme of those messages wasn't worry.

"No, Mom," he said. *"You're* worried, and you don't have to be. Bella is—"

She was everything.

Simple as that.

But also, she made things exceptionally complicated. It had been him and his mom for so long that he didn't know what she'd do without him. Hell, he still went over once a week and mowed her lawn, and the last time there'd been a power outage, she hadn't known where the breakers were.

"Fancy switches," she'd called them.

But it was more than that, more than the man-of-the-house stuff. His mom was alone, and if he was busy with his own life, then what would she do?

"Oh no," she said, glaring at him. "Wipe that look off your face right now. I'm a grown woman, and I don't need my son to look after me." She sighed and her expression softened. "I already allowed that to go on for too long. I took advantage of you, Henry, relied on you too much, stole you away and kept you home when I should have been pushing you to go back to New York."

"I *wanted* to stay."

"No. You felt like you *had* to stay." She slipped down from the stool, crossed over to him. "That was my fault. I—"

"Maybe at first I didn't want to be here," he admitted. "But I love this town, Mom. I couldn't imagine living anywhere else."

"And if this *Bella* decides that small-town life isn't for her?"

"That's not an issue."

"It could become one."

He shrugged. "If it does, then we'll figure it out. Together," he added when it seemed as though she'd protest.

"Your mom is right to worry," came a quiet voice.

Both of their gazes shot to the doorway. Bella stood in the hall, eyes warm but expression careful.

"It's a mother's job to worry about her baby."

Henry groaned.

Because that was probably the only thing Bella could have said to put his mother at ease.

It was, in fact, one of his mom's favorite statements.

Case in point, the beaming smile that spread across her face. "Exactly. Please come in, dear," she said. "I'm Catherine."

"Isabella," Bella replied as she walked into the room, arms laden with bags.

She'd been sweet-talking the local farmers for extra produce and it looked as though today she'd scored—he took the bags from her—apricots.

The sweet smell hit his nose and promptly made his mouth water.

She kissed him on the cheek, murmured a soft, "Thank you." Then, arms free, turned to his mother. "It's so lovely to finally meet you, Catherine. How was your cruise?" She smiled at his mom's surprised expression. "I hope you don't mind, but Henry showed me a few pictures of your travels. It looked absolutely beautiful."

"It was wonderful," his mother said. "And I've been hearing all about you and your wonderful desserts since I got back. I'm happy to say your blueberry cobbler far surpasses the hype."

Bella whirled around to face him. "You did *not* feed your mother my reject cobbler!"

Henry shrugged helplessly. He'd been between a rock and a hard place and plus, the *reject cobbler* was fucking delicious.

"Hush now." His mom wove her arm through Bella's, thus saving him from his woman's wrath. "Henry's father was just the same way, not liking anyone to taste until the recipe was just perfect." She started tugging Bella into the family room. "But I'll tell you what I used to tell him. Sometimes, the perfection is found in the mistakes."

Bella froze for a moment then smiled down at his mom. "You know what? You're absolutely right."

Approximately one minute later, they were giggling together on his couch.

He snapped a pic with his cell, sent it to Kel.

Traitor.

She replied within a few seconds.

I had to do something. Plus, it looks like they're thick as thieves already. Should I be jealous?

He rolled his eyes.

You turned me down, remember?

A beat.

Oh, I remember. So when can I meet her? Or better yet, when are you going to bring her to the ranch so I can get her on a horse? Theo's out because he's strictly Melissa's horse now. But I have others.

Henry stifled a chuckle.

Too many others, according to Justin.

His phone buzzed again.

Lies.

He smirked.

Maybe. Maybe not. How about Monday?

A heartbeat before her reply came through.

Monday is good. I promise not to cook.

Henry shook his head as he picked up the phone and called in an order for a pizza. Based on the amount of cackling, he anticipated their conversation was going to take a while.

His mom was sharing baby stories.

"And then he whipped off his undies and streaked off down the aisle, his little butt jiggling as he ran. He was so fast and more slippery than a greased hog. I just couldn't catch him—"

Bella burst out laughing, and his mom joined in.

For fuck's sake.

But Henry couldn't hold back his smile when he joined them on the couch.

He would endure any amount of embarrassment if it made the two most important women in his life laugh like that.

FOURTEEN

Bella

"SO LOVELY TO MEET YOU again, my dear," Catherine murmured, pulling Bella down for a tight hug.

Henry's mom really was tiny . . . or maybe it was just that Bella was too tall?

Either way, she had to stoop down to receive the hug.

So worth it, though, she thought as Catherine gave her the perfect Mom Hug. Tight, but not too much so, long enough to show she cared, but not so prolonged that it drifted into the creepy sector.

Just . . . perfect.

God, she missed her own mom.

Shoving that thought away, she hugged Catherine back. "You don't have to go," she said for what must have been the fifth time in as many minutes. "I know you just got back from your trip and must want to see—"

"Pish." A wide smile as she stepped back. "I'll pester him tomorrow. For now, you two lovebirds enjoy your evening together."

The three of them had chatted for the better part of an hour before the doorbell had rung and the pizza Henry had ordered appeared. There was enough for the three of them to share, but Catherine had refused to stay.

"But you haven't eaten," Bella said, not wanting Henry's mom to feel like she was being run off.

Catherine patted her hips. "I've eaten more than enough over the last few weeks. Plus, I had your delicious cobbler." Her lips tipped up into a smile that was very much like Henry's. "Pretend I'm living vicariously and having dessert for dinner," she mock-whispered.

Bella giggled.

"Talk to you both soon," Catherine called, showing herself out the front door before Bella could force her to stay for pizza. She watched through the window as Henry's mom walked to her car, got in, and drove away.

Apparently, she wasn't the only one watching.

The moment his mom's car was out of sight, Henry's arms were around Bella's waist, and he was tugging her back against his chest.

"I missed you."

She scoffed, turned in his embrace to snuggle closer. "We were apart for all of two hours."

"Two hours too long." A roll of her eyes, but because his eyes were sparkling with humor, she didn't tease him. Especially when he pressed a kiss to her temple and asked, "Where'd you get the apricots?"

"You wouldn't believe it if I told you," she said and launched into the crazy story about the farmer and his runaway dog she'd corralled outside the apartment. "Thank God I got the new cell phone because he was just sitting there on my stoop, paws crossed and the saddest expression on his face. And when I opened the door, he just ran inside. Luckily for him, he had tags. I called and . . ."

Had ended up with four full bags of ripe and juicy apricots.

"I don't know how much pizza I can eat," she confessed. "I think I ate a half dozen apricots just on the walk over here."

Henry grinned, nuzzling the side of her throat and leaving goose bumps in his wake. "There's a dirty joke somewhere in there."

"Leave it hidden," she quipped, but the words weren't exactly steady.

He spun her to face him. "So you're not hungry?"

She shook her head.

"Does that mean I can kiss you now?"

Bella didn't justify that question with a response. Instead, she rose on tiptoe, wrapped her arms around his neck, and kissed him.

His reaction was instantaneous.

One second, she was in control, the next she found herself lifted onto the kitchen counter, his hard cock pressing against her and his tongue darting into her mouth in a rhythm that had her seeing stars.

God, they'd done so much kissing over the last two weeks, taking it slow, but also driving her insane by increments.

Her body remembered what it had been like between them.

Her heart wanted to be close to him like that again.

Even her brain said go for it.

But when she snaked her hand down, grappling with the button on his jeans, he caught it, pulled back from the kiss, and smiled down at her.

"Dangerous." One more smack of his lips against hers, before he started to reach for the pizza box. "We really should eat this before it gets cold."

Bella saw red. She pulled away from him and stomped her foot. "Are you kidding me?"

His lips twitched, and her anger swiveled into irritation.

Though, truthfully, it was nice to see the glimpse of the old Henry. The one who teased her and drove her crazy and didn't treat her like a piece of fragile glass. Because while, yes, they had spent the majority of the past weeks together, while they'd kissed and touched and held each other, there had been a careful distance between them.

As though Henry were waiting for something.

For her to leave again.

Or maybe . . . for her to prove she wouldn't.

He tucked a strand of hair behind her ear. "But, yes, I *am* kidding."

Bella shot him a mock-frown. "Not. Funny."

"From where I'm standing it is." He grinned when her mock-frown turned real. "Sure you don't want to just eat pizza and watch a movie?"

The same thing they'd done more often than not. Oh, they'd gone out and watched a movie in the local theater, in addition to sitting through a few more sunsets at his spot. They'd even played a game of miniature golf that she was absolutely terrible at. But most of the nights had involved food and just spending time together.

Now that the heavy topics had been dealt with, they'd been able to chat about all the fun stuff.

Fancy ingredients, jerky head chefs, favorite reality shows.

Places they wanted to visit.

Not Italy, for her part. Oh, she loved the country she'd grown up in, but it had felt like a prison so much over the years that the thought of going back did *not* appeal. Then there was the fact that it would bring her closer to her father.

Not preferred.

He'd remotely shut down her laptop and cell, canceled her credit cards, closed her checking account. Bella now had no funds, aside from what she earned at the diner, and one suitcase of clothes to her name. Thankfully, she wasn't on a visa—she was a dual citizen, since she'd been born in the States and her mother had been an American—because if Bella *had* been, her father certainly would have found a way to make her life miserable.

For the first time in her life, she was truly on her own.

Which was perfectly okay with her, if not for the fact that she kept waiting for the other shoe to fall.

For her father to find some string to pull.

But she wouldn't dance to his tune. Not this time. He had nothing to hold over her head and—

"I was kidding about eating the pizza."

The husky words startled her out of her thoughts.

She blinked. "Pardon?"

"Did I ruin the moment?"

"N-no," she stammered, trying to get her mind to clear. "Thinking about my father did that."

Henry made a face.

"Sorry. Sorry. I just—" Bella pursed her lips. "Ruined the moment."

He grabbed the box of pizza, picked up her hand again, and tugged her down the hall to his bedroom.

Figuring it was best to keep her mouth shut after she'd spent the last few minutes off in dreamland, before mentioning the libido-killing subject of her father, she just followed along.

He didn't stop until they'd reached the bed.

Once there, he tossed the pizza on it, turned back, and bent, pulling off his shoes. Hers went by the wayside next. Then Henry whipped off his shirt.

"Uh." Not that she was complaining.

"Shh," he said, unbuttoning his jeans and pushing them down.

That wasn't hard, considering the way her mouth had gone dry at the sight of all that naked skin. His chest was lickable, and her fingers actually tingled with the urge to touch his abs or maybe stroke down the muscles of his arms or maybe . . . *okay*, she wanted to touch him everywhere.

He slipped his fingers under the hem of her T-shirt and tugged it up and over her head then helped her shimmy out of her jeans.

And then he stopped and grabbed the TV remote.

Her brows yanked together, throat unsticking. Yes, the view of him bending over was yummy, but she'd rather him be bending for a reason that was not turning on a television.

Like bending so that his mouth was between her legs.

Yup, *that* she could get behind.

Before she could suggest that, he started streaming an old romantic comedy and set the remote down. *Okaay*. Five years had passed. Maybe he was into some weird, kinky stuff now?

Like old romcoms featuring fake orgasm scenes and heroines with beautifully curly hair.

Unbidden, Bella reached up to straighten her ponytail. *Her* hair didn't hold a curl. *It* would never look like that—

She squealed as Henry swept her up into his arms.

Her mind flickered, losing focus when all that hot naked skin pressed against hers.

"What are you—?"

"I'm getting you out of your head," he said, setting her down on the mattress, following her down so that full length of him was over the top of her. *Fuck, that was nice.* He nuzzled her neck. "We've got pizza. We're sort of watching a movie. So you can just relax and focus on you." His mouth tipped up. "Or rather, on *us*."

She raised a brow. "Naked?"

"If that's what you want," he said, amusement curling through the words.

"You seem to have gotten us there with very little effort."

He stroked one hand along the outside of her thigh, up her hip, her rib cage, and stopped, fingertips teasing the sensitive skin just below her breast.

She shivered.

"You cold?"

A roll of her eyes. "You know that's not why I have goose bumps."

"Yeah?" He brushed his mouth along her jaw, down her throat.

"Y—" He nipped the spot just above her collarbone, and her hands wove into his hair, arching closer, needing— "Yes."

His tongue darted out, sliding down until it traced along the top edge of her bra . . . so damn close and yes, so freaking far from where she wanted him. "Then why?" He nudged the cotton out of the way, grazed the hardened bud of her nipple, and she jumped, heat pooling in her stomach, her thighs clenching together.

And that was enough.

She could hardly remember what they were talking about, could barely remember her name.

She wanted him.

She wanted Henry.

Now.

Enough teasing. Enough taking it slow. Just . . . enough. She wrapped her legs around his waist and yanked him down, so his lower half was firmly pressed against hers. Bella got one glimpse of his expression—proud and self-satisfied that he'd gotten her out of her own brain, no doubt—before she gripped his head and brought his mouth to hers.

She couldn't fault the man for his smugness.

His plan had worked after all.

But now it was *her* job to drive him slowly insane.

FIFTEEN

Henry

HE WAS LOSING his fucking mind.

Bella was beneath him, legs around his hips, his cock pressed against her pussy, and only two layers of thin material separating him from the motherland.

And she was wet.

So much so that he could feel it soaking through his boxer briefs.

This was supposed to be about driving *her* crazy, getting her so turned on that she didn't have the mental space to think about anything except the two of them and how good it felt for them to be together. He'd wanted to get her out of her brain and far away from the worries that had left shadows in her eyes.

Yes, Sergio was gone.

No, her father hadn't contacted her, aside from decisively cutting her off from him in every way he could, but luckily Henry's woman was smart and a hard-worker. She'd more than earned the wages at the diner, had insisted on paying him rent, refused to let him buy her a new cell phone. She—

Kissed him.

And then *his* mental space emptied.

No more thoughts of fathers or exes. Nothing except sensation and need and raging, all-encompassing desire. He slipped his tongue into her mouth, let his hips drop more firmly against hers, making them both groan.

She nipped his bottom lip, and he nipped back.

Then reached beneath her back to unhook her bra. Two seconds later, she'd slipped her arms free and tossed the garment aside before tugging his head down to her breasts.

Fuck, yes.

He probably should have eased into it, teased her slowly, but the sight of her hardened nipples was too much. He sucked one into his mouth, drawing deeply and loving the way her hands wove into his hair to hold him there.

His other hand slid up her ribs, wanting to tease her other nipple, to caress her breast, but he couldn't get the angle he wanted without crushing her.

One quick movement had their positions reversed, Bella's delicious breasts swaying in front of his mouth. Henry didn't hesitate, just ratcheted up, seized her breasts in his hands, and got to work, alternating between his lips and teeth and tongue, pinching and circling the stiff peaks, reveling in the way she cried and arched against him.

"*Oh God,*" she groaned, undulating against him.

The two layers between them that had been so thin and tempting before now created an uncomfortable sort of friction. It was a nuisance that he wanted gone.

Skin to skin.

Sliding home.

Delving deep.

His cock went painfully hard.

Bella moved against him, pelvis rocking faster, the rhythm

making stars flash behind his eyes, his mouth faltered on her breasts. He moved his hands to her ass, shifting her slightly, holding her tight, and her breath caught.

"H-Henry."

Desire had him hardened to a fever pitch, but he knew that tone, knew that she was close.

She started to slow her movements, probably wanting to wait for him.

Well, *fuck that.*

She was beautiful when she came.

And it had been five years too many since he'd seen it.

He pulled her more firmly against him, sped her movements so that her breath caught . . . then transformed into a moan.

"I—"

He leaned up, took her nipple into his mouth, and sucked deeply.

"*Oh.*" Her lips parted, and she threw her head back. Fuck, it was the most beautiful thing he'd ever seen. Pink staining her cheeks, eyes slammed closed, lips parted on a moan as she moved faster and harder . . . until—

"Mmm. Oh my God. *Henry.*"

She shattered, her orgasm having her stiffen for one long moment before she collapsed against him, hips still moving, her groan of pleasure the sexiest thing he'd ever heard.

"Fuck," she murmured, lips to his shoulder, body limp. "Just fuck."

He grinned, gave her exactly ten seconds to catch her breath, then flipped her over onto her back and dove between her thighs.

She shrieked, but by the time she'd recovered herself enough to protest, Henry had her underwear off, her legs spread, and his mouth on her clit. *Gently,* because she'd just come, but he circled the nub with his tongue, sucking lightly, stroking his fingers through her folds.

Soaking wet.

Hot, liquid heat.

So. Fucking. Gorgeous.

He stroked slowly at first, building her back up, enjoying the sweetness of her against his taste buds. He knew she liked firm pressure against her clit, so the moment she could take it, he flattened his tongue and circled the bundle of nerves, teasing her until she cursed at him and then, biting back a smirk, he gave her what she really wanted.

Hard and fast and demanding.

He slipped a finger inside, curling it up against her G-spot while sucking deeply on her clit.

Within seconds, she was writhing, hips jerking, moans coming in rapid succession, but he rode the wave with her, bringing her higher and higher until she screamed his name and tightened around his finger.

She flopped back on the mattress, chest heaving. It did all sorts of wonderful things to her breasts that he was having trouble ignoring, since his cock was still rock-hard, but he wasn't an asshole. He didn't expect anything from Bella in return. He sure as fuck hoped for it, but he didn't expect—

Her hand snaked down, gripping him through the damp fabric of his boxer briefs.

His groan was garbled, and his hips shot up, cock seeking more of her.

Hand. Mouth. Pussy.

He almost didn't care.

Except, who was he kidding.

Henry was desperate to be inside her again, but he also knew it was important for her to have control after spending so long without it.

Her fingers ran down the length of him. Back up.

Down. Up.

Driving him slowly insane.

"Henry?" she murmured.

He gritted his teeth. The heroine faking an orgasm on the TV behind him wasn't helping his control in the least. He just kept thinking about how much he liked the sound of Bella as she came. "Hmm?" he replied.

"Are you going to get inside me?" she asked. "Or are you just the ultimate tease?"

His eyes flew open. He hadn't even known he'd slammed them shut.

But Bella's question had them flashing wide then promptly stifling a curse as he tried not to embarrass himself. She was naked and spread out beneath him, her breasts on full display, and while she'd dropped her hand from his cock, she'd wrapped her legs around his hips in its place.

One layer of fabric between them.

It was not enough.

It was too much.

She arched, bringing their pelvises into perfect alignment. "Are you going to make love to me, Henry?" she asked. "Or do I need to distract *your* mind?"

He could barely process her words he was so turned on. "I —" He broke off on a groan when she shimmied against him, and the devil woman had the nerve to smile sweetly up at him, mischief dancing in her eyes.

"Distracted enough?"

Another movement that had sweat breaking out along his spine.

"So. Fucking. Dangerous," he growled, having at least retained enough presence of mind to reach over her and pull out a condom from his nightstand drawer.

A heartbeat later, he'd torn it open with his teeth.

One more to strip off his boxer briefs. Another to roll it down his length.

He paused, lungs tight, heart pounding.

"Yes," she murmured.

And he couldn't have waited another second to be inside her.

Slowly, Henry slid home, jaw clenching at the perfectness of her. Wet and tight and hot, it was almost too much. But it had also been too long. He wanted to savor her, appreciate the way she felt, the way being like this with her made *him* feel. He wanted—

She tightened around him. "Move, Henry."

Savoring was suddenly the last thing on his mind.

He pulled out, pushed back in, tilting his hips so he rubbed against her clit while also hitting her G-spot. Yes, he was chasing an orgasm that was already prickling on the edges of his consciousness, but fuck if he was going to allow himself to fall over the precipice without Bella coming at least one more time.

Her fingers dug in his shoulders, a moan escaping her lips.

Yup. That was the spot she liked.

And he liked the motion, too. *Way* too fucking much.

Because his best intentions or not, his orgasm was coming

Too fast. Too fast.

He didn't realize he'd spoken the chant aloud until Bella cupped his cheek and said, "No, baby. More. *Faster.*"

The leash on his control snapped.

Henry *moved*. In and out, faster and faster, until her Bella was groaning and moving against him, coaxing him on and then ... finally—*thank God because he was so fucking close*—she stiffened and cried out, tightening around him.

That was it for him.

One stroke. Two. And he exploded.

SIXTEEN

Bella

SHE WAS HUMMING as she worked in the kitchen, slicing the apricots she'd gotten from Jim and throwing them into a pot to cook down into a compote.

Bella was going to break her own rule by staying over at Henry's place.

He was getting dressed so he could drive her home.

Ridiculous man.

She'd rented the apartment for a reason. Before tonight she had made herself go back home, no matter how late her and Henry's time together went, because she'd thought it important to have some distance between them as they got to know each other again.

Tonight had shown her that was a joke.

Keeping him at arm's length when they worked side by side and spent every waking moment together was impossible.

And then there was the fact that she didn't *want* there to be space between them.

Maybe it wasn't the most prudent decision, maybe she'd end

up with a broken heart in the end, but Bella also felt like she had wasted enough time. Who knew how long she had on this earth?

She wanted whatever time she had to be spent with Henry.

Plus, he insisted on driving her home every time, even though the distance between the house and apartment was only a few blocks.

Equal parts sweet and infuriating.

Sweet because he cared, because he kissed her so gently at her front door.

Infuriating because she'd left an abusive relationship, flown halfway around the world, and started a new life. She didn't *need* him to drive her home.

But, her brain countered, he didn't need *her* to cook for him.

Well, she cooked because she cared, because it was one way for her to show it.

Bella wrinkled her nose, knowing that Henry's driving her home was along the same vein. It was obvious, logical, but she didn't want her brain to be logical or mature.

She wanted to pout.

A hand snuck onto her cutting board, stole a sliver of apricot.

"I thought I was going to drive you home."

She turned, pointed the knife at him. "Not anymore. Get the blue cheese out of the fridge. I have homemade crackers in the oven."

He hesitated, eyes drifting down to the end of her knife.

Then he shrugged, but Bella saw his lips twitch before he turned and dug out the cheese. After he'd set it next to her, the oven dinged, and he glanced inside before she could ask him to check on the crackers.

"Another minute," he murmured, pressing a kiss to the side of her neck and snagging another apricot off her board.

She sighed but held up another piece.

He ate it, nipping at her fingertips and making the space between her thighs clench.

Three orgasms, she reminded her vagina. *Just chill already.*

But it didn't want to *chill.* It wanted Henry again.

Bella gave an internal snort. When had her vagina become autonomous? Because it wasn't just that she desired Henry or that she really loved it when he pounded into her, his cock hard and deep. Nope. *She* wanted him.

Every part of her.

Which was why she announced, "I'm staying."

He froze, tray hovering, crackers stalled mid-retrieval. After a moment, he blinked, extracted the sheet pan, and set it carefully on the counter.

"I don't mind driving—"

"I'm. Staying," she growled, grabbing a piece of apricot and shoving it into her mouth.

First, he complained about driving her home. Now he wanted her to go.

What the fuck?

"Fine," she snapped, slamming down her knife. "I'll go."

Hands on her waist, lifting her and plunking her down on the opposite counter, well away from the sharp blade and simmering pot on the stove. Henry nudged her thighs apart, stepped between them. At which point, her vagina decided it was time to party, or rather, that it wanted to party with Henry's cock, but Bella knew she needed to hold it together.

Why? her vagina cajoled. *You like it.*

Well, there was *that* argument. She did. She really—

"I don't want you to go."

Bella glanced up at him, eyes widening. "What?"

He smiled. "You heard me."

"But—"

"I've been pestering you to stay," he said. "You don't

honestly think that because you'd surprised me with your proclamation that I don't want you to stay, do you?"

Her mouth opened. Closed.

"Or maybe you're worried that because we've had sex that something has changed?"

"Something *has* changed," she grumbled.

"Has it?" he asked. "Or are you just feeling vulnerable?"

Ugh. How did this man always know exactly what she was feeling? She didn't want to feel vulnerable. She *wanted* to feel like she did before. All happy and orgasm-drugged and—

"That's it, isn't it?" he teased. "My brave, tough, gorgeous Isabella is scared."

She pushed at his chest. "Shut up," she snapped, but even as the sharp words penetrated the air between them, Henry just continued to smile. The jerk actually kept smiling. "Back up," she said, shoving him again. "I need to get the crackers off the tray and check on the—"

He didn't budge.

She sighed, stared at his rather lovely kitchen. Pale gray cabinets, white countertops, a double oven, and a big eight-burner stove.

"Sweetheart." Henry cupped her cheek and waited until she finally brought her eyes back to his. "I love you."

Her breath caught.

Hearing those words never got old.

"I'll drive you home." A kiss to her forehead. "Or not." Another to her cheek. "You can stay." Her other cheek. "Or not." He brushed his mouth across hers. "Don't you see? I just want you, sweetheart. Wherever or whenever or in however much you're willing to give."

"I—"

She sniffed.

Henry sniffed.

They both reacted at once, darting over to the pan on the stove. He pulled it off the heat and shot her a sheepish grin.

"My compote!" Bella glared at him, but she couldn't stay mad, not when he looked at her like that. She sighed, lips turning down into a frown. "It's ruined."

He swiped a finger into the pan, licked off the burned fruit mixture, and winced.

"Yup. It's ruined."

She shook her head, exasperated, but feeling decidedly less flayed open. Because of Henry. Because he'd pestered and annoyed and cajoled her into realizing that he was vulnerable, too, that his emotions were as big and scary as her own.

That he wanted her to stay but supported her if she went.

Another piece of her heart was imprinted with Henry's name.

The man kept saying *she* was dangerous.

Well, *he* was the one who kept snatching parts of her soul, taking them and transforming them into something more, transforming *her* into a different person.

One she liked a whole hell of a lot.

One he loved, even with her grumbling and snapping and—

He spun her around, pressed a hard kiss to her mouth. "Plus, if you're going to stay, we can make another batch." A smile that stole her breath. "That's the thing about second chances. We have the opportunity to make them even better than the first time around."

Bella stayed.

And she made another batch of compote.

And, Henry was right.

It was even better.

SEVENTEEN

Henry

MONDAY NIGHT WAS BEAUTIFUL. One of those perfect summer nights where the air was warm, but a light breeze prevented anyone from getting too hot.

The kids were out in full force. Max and Allie, Rob and Melissa's kids, felt it was their duty as the older cousins to lead little Abigail astray. Or in this particular case, through an obstacle course of blocks, jump ropes, and chairs. Even the twins, who were toddling like crazy over the lawn to keep up with their cousins, tried desperately to get in on the action.

Bella watched the activity with a smile on her face.

She'd won over Kelly and Justin easily, coming prepared with a tray of apricot cobbler—Henry had talked to the farmer and now she was inundated with the small orange fruit—and a huge layered chocolate cake that the kids had gaped over.

Melissa had crossed her arms upon seeing the desserts, sending Bella a mock-glare whose intensity was tempered by the amusement in her pale brown eyes. "You'll have me out of my job in no time."

"Never," Bella had replied before her cheeks went pink. "I have to admit that I have all of your cookbooks."

And another one bit the dust.

Melissa had taken the tray from Henry then lead Bella into the huge kitchen of the main house. It was where her cooking show was filmed and where, in fact, the producer asked if he could have the cameraman, who was at the house to film some additional scenes that would be edited into shows later in the season, take some shots of the desserts.

Bella had agreed and then pretty soon she was talking about her cake on camera, bubbly and confident and charming everyone in sight.

First Esther. Then the town. Him. His mother. His best friend. Television producers.

When would it stop?

Henry smothered a grin. Probably not until she achieved world domination.

"It's really nice to see you so happy."

He turned and saw Kelly with Jessie on her hip. She reached for him, so he swung her up into his arms.

"Rocket ship!" she yelled.

He groaned.

Kel laughed.

And speaking of it being really nice to see someone happy. He was thrilled that his best friend had found someone like Justin. Unlike his twin brother, Rex, who was the biological father of Abigail and a royal asshole, Justin was a good guy.

Rex, on the other hand, had taken advantage of a lonely Kelly, knocked her up, then skipped town.

Of course, Kel had forgiven him. Especially after Rex had terminated his parental rights, thus allowing Justin to formally adopt Abigail.

Justin had been there for Abby and Kel almost from day

one, and the little girl knew no other father. He was a good one, too. Engaged, funny, kind, and caring. And though he was quieter than Henry's own dad had been, there was something about Justin that reminded him of his dad.

Loyal. Always had his back.

He watched Justin swoop in and grab Jax before the little boy—who'd somehow managed to scale a fence post—fell to the ground.

A quick word, an even quicker squeeze, and the toddler was on his way again.

Case in point.

A tug on his ear brought his attention back to Jessie. She was frowning at him. "Rocket ship!" she repeated.

Henry did a quick round of math. Five kiddos. Two of which were getting too damned big for rocket ships, but who still would definitely want them. One back that wasn't getting any younger.

"Just two," he told her.

Tiny lips pursing as they considered his deal then a nod.

"Two," she agreed.

Kel smirked. "I'll help Miss bring the plates out. Maybe by then you'll have thrown your back out."

"Why are we friends again?" He huffed, lowering Jessie to the ground in preparation for takeoff.

"Because I'm awesome." She turned for the house. "And my kids love you."

"Thee. Two. One!" Jessie shouted, still working on her R's.

Henry knew what she meant anyway and rocketed her high into the sky. Which was all it took for four pairs of child-sized feet to pound his way. Their voices layered over one another, each demanding their own turn, until finally, Jessie declared firmly and loud enough to be heard over the cacophony, "Two each."

Surprisingly, the kids all agreed and sat down for their turn.

After the tenth and final takeoff, Henry collapsed on the grass. "Who's going to give *me* a rocket ship?"

There was a pause before Jax said, "Daddy!"

Henry laughed and gave Jax a fist bump. "I think you're right, bud. He's the only one strong enough to lift me."

The kids nodded in solemn agreement before Kel's voice rang out over the lawn, announcing dinner was ready and ordering them all to wash up. At the prospect of food in the near future, they took off, leaving him a limp pile of exhaustion in the grass.

"You're really good with them."

He'd known Bella was there, felt the prickle of awareness on his nape, the skip of his pulse.

She extended a hand, a silent offer to help him to his feet.

He placed his fingers in hers, tugged hard.

"Eek!" She squealed, plopping down on top of him. The elbow he received on her landing was probably well-deserved, but it was also why it took him a moment to catch his breath.

"Hey," he said, wrapping his arms around her, keeping her close when she tried to get up.

"We—"

He kissed her.

She stopped trying to push off him and kissed him back. It was affection mixed with exasperation, longing with a dash of tempered heat. Sweet and soft and almost soothing, but with just the slightest edge of desire that had his pulse pounding.

A shriek penetrated his brain, jarring him enough that he pulled back.

Bella's eyes were closed, her lips red and swollen.

"Do you want kids?"

Because he could picture a little girl with the same espresso eyes, identical brown hair.

Her eyes flashed open, mouth working for a few seconds before she actually got the words out. "Of course, I do," she said. "Someday in the future, for sure." She glanced over at the front door of the main house when another happy yell reached their ears. The door was wide open, the threshold empty, the kiddos having disappeared inside. And by the sound of it, they were having a great time washing up. "Henry, we should—"

"One more minute," he said and kissed her again.

She melted against him, one minute turning into more like five, or maybe ten.

The second time they pulled apart wasn't due to a kid, but rather because of Kel's mom voice. Turned out she had a really good one.

Or, at least knew the exact right threat to get Henry moving.

"Hey, love birds," Kel yelled from the front door. "You have exactly one minute before I'm setting the twins on you. They're hungry and impatient, and *you know* how they feel about Aunt Melissa's homemade mac and cheese."

Henry shuddered. The twins liked to eat.

They also redefined the word hangry. Hevil was more like it.

"Coming," he called, shifting Bella off him and shooting her a sheepish smile as he stood. Her hair was a disaster, the pony-tail having come halfway loose, tendrils falling all over the place. He extended a hand down to her, tugged her to her feet, wondering if he should offer to get some of the grass out of her hair or off her clothes or her—

She sighed, brushing herself off before lifting the hem of her T-shirt away from her body and shaking it.

Little pieces of grass fluttered to the ground.

Accusatory eyebrows in his direction.

Note to self, rolling around on the lawn got a lot more complicated when he had roving hands.

Next was her ponytail, sliding the band free, shaking out her hair for a few quick seconds before sweeping it right back up into the holder's tight grip. He'd watched her do the same thing a hundred times when they'd been together in the past, but seeing her do it today reminded him how grateful he was to have this second chance.

To have her here with his friends. To have her in Darlington at the diner. To know his mom loved her as much as he did.

The only bittersweet part was that his dad wasn't there.

Henry knew that feeling would never completely go away, but after having discovered what Bella had gone through to help his father, without even knowing him. Finding out that she'd sacrificed everything to give him one final chance . . . she had to know that she absolutely owned Henry—heart, soul, fingers, toes.

Every piece of him belonged to her.

One quick tug to her ponytail and she turned back to him, coming close enough to rest her hands on his chest, rising on tiptoe to press a quick kiss to his cheek.

"Come on, my sweet, troublesome man."

Dropping to her heels, she snagged his hand.

And Henry knew that though this was the beginning, everything would be all right.

EIGHTEEN

Bella

A FEW DAYS LATER, she found herself alone in the diner.

She'd just turned off the lights, all the staff had finished their rounds of cleaning and sweeping and restocking tables, and Henry had zipped off to help Tilly, who'd gotten a flat a few miles out of town.

Bella had ordered him to go, knowing there was prep work to do for the following morning and also wanting to get a head start on some baking.

There was a real wedding at the Roosevelt Ranch this weekend.

She'd gotten to see the space at dinner the other evening. The new pavilion and gazebo had just received the finishing touches—twinkly lights everywhere, beds of brightly colored flowers, rows of coordinating gingham topped hay bales with thick pads carefully concealed so guests' bottoms wouldn't get poked. Mason jars and tea lights and horseshoes and cowboy boots.

They'd thought of everything.

And now completed, it was more gorgeous in person than the pictures she'd drooled over a couple of months ago on their website.

Probably more importantly, or at least more importantly to *her*, was the fact that Bella got to make the wedding cake. Initially, Melissa was going to do the honors and film the process for her show, but the bride had gotten camera shy on Monday morning, and so they were scrambling to draw up a new idea for the episode.

Melissa had still offered to make the cake, not wanting the couple to not have one, but then over bowls of delicious mac and cheese, Kelly had suggested that maybe Bella could make it.

"Could you really?" Melissa had asked, relief creeping into the edges of her expression. "I can do it, but I'm not a pastry chef. I've seen the things you've made"—she'd pointed at the chocolate cake that was sitting under a mesh dome in the center of the outdoor dining table—"case in point, that gorgeous confection. I could meet with you and the bride and—"

Bella had put her hand on the other woman's arm. "I'm happy to help, however you need."

And she meant it.

There was something different about this town, about the people in it. Not only did Darlington look after their own, but they freely offered up help without expecting anything in return.

Offers to help her carrying in groceries to her apartment, boxes into the diner. Rides to Henry's house if she was walking from downtown.

Frankly, it had been unnerving at first.

But she'd quickly learned that was the way Darlington worked.

She'd watched Esther scoop up a crying baby in the diner, bouncing him around the tables so his frazzled mom could eat.

Henry had left to change a tire with nary a second thought. Melissa had offered her the chance—and the payment she'd been going to receive—to make a wedding cake.

The town was wonderful.

Oh, there was the occasional jerk or curmudgeon or stupid teenager. In fact, Rob, Melissa's husband, had her in hysterics at dinner on Monday as he'd described trying to figure out who had been stealing mailboxes from the neighborhood and putting them all on Mr. Watson's—one well-known Darlington curmudgeon—lawn.

So different from home when she'd been sequestered on the estate, lonely except for the internet and books.

So different from New York, which had been exciting and different and filled to the brim with noises and scents and people.

She really liked it here.

And while it had only been a few weeks, Bella couldn't imagine living anywhere else.

She hummed as she worked, dicing up peppers and onions and carefully stowing them in the walk-in. Next came shredding cheese, making sure there were enough eggs and flour and baking soda.

Breakfast service was always busy, and the town loved Henry's omelets and pancakes.

Speaking of which, she went ahead and mixed up some pancake batter. It wouldn't hurt to sit overnight, though it might require some thinning in the morning since the flour molecules tended to tighten up, thus thickening the mixture, over time. Still, it would save Frank a step.

Pulling out her phone, she sent him a picture, letting him know it was there for him in the fridge, then washed up.

The soft chime of her cell signaling Frank's reply had her frowning.

She hadn't remembered turning it off silent.

Shrugging, she wiped her hands on her apron and turned for the shelves holding the dried goods. Henry still wasn't back from fixing Tilly's tire, so she figured she might as well get a head start on the wedding cake.

The bride, Shelby, wanted four tiers, all with different flavors—chocolate-peanut butter, lemon-coconut, vanilla, and salted caramel—and Bella was beyond excited to get started. The actual design would be simple, no topsy-turvy stacking or thousands of gum paste flowers. Which was a good thing because the wedding was in two days, and though Henry and Frank had both offered to help, their strong suit wasn't in crafting edible flowers. Not to mention, the diner wasn't exactly designed for baking. Oh, there were commercial ovens, along with heat and humidity that would wreak havoc on fondant, gum paste, and chocolate.

Still, she had cake pans and all the necessary ingredients to at least get the cakes baked. Melissa had sent her the recipes the bride had taste-tested and chosen, so she didn't have to start from scratch.

But, she couldn't help herself from making a little tweak here or there.

Today, she was starting with the chocolate peanut butter.

Melissa's recipe called for peanut butter chips in the batter, Bella had a little trick to bypass that.

She ground her own peanuts into butter, added local, organic honey, and thinned the mixture with a little milk. Then she swirled it into the pan with the chocolate batter so the two flavors would be more evenly mixed.

Using a small pan at first, she prepared the two components, swirled them together, and slid it in the oven.

Then she set about making some buttercream frosting that she'd freeze and later thaw to cover the outside of the cake. By the time that was finished and stowed safely away, the cake smelled done.

A press to its middle, another long sniff, and she let it stay in for two more minutes as she stacked dirty dishes into the sink.

Her stomach rumbled when she pulled out the pan.

"Oh, yes," she murmured. "You're absolutely perfect, aren't you?"

"I used to say the same thing about you."

Bella whipped around, saw who was in the doorway, and dropped the pan.

The hot cake broke into pieces, burning her legs through her jeans, her feet through her shoes.

But she barely felt it, not with the terror gripping her so tightly.

Her eyes darted around, searching for an exit even though she knew she was trapped.

Still, she had to try to get away.

They stepped into the kitchen.

Heart pounding, she waved a hand to the stools Henry kept along one wall. "Why don't you sit down?"

And then, when their gazes slid to the line of chairs, Bella made a run for it.

NINETEEN

Henry

THE OLD IDIOM, no good deed went unpunished, was proving to be true.

Henry hadn't minded coming to help Tilly, not when it was dark and she had told him she hadn't been able to get a hold of Trent, who owned the only tow truck in town.

But that was an hour ago.

Before he knew the tire was a stubborn asshole that wasn't going to cooperate. First, the lug nut had jammed, then the jack hadn't wanted to work. Then just as he bent near the car to retighten the bolts, some jerkwad in a huge black SUV had sped down the dimly light road, nearly mowing him and Tilly over.

"Not local," he muttered, making sure to give a better look out for traffic as he knelt next to the car again.

"Probably from the wedding," Tilly said. "Out of towners always drive like crazy people."

"They don't know about the murderous deer," he quipped, making her laugh.

The thought made his lips twitch, remembering how the

story of Haley and Sam's run-ins with the numerous deer on this road—two motor accidents that had resulted in two totaled cars and one broken ankle . . . and no injuries to the deer themselves—had reached Bella over in Italy.

He tightened the lug nuts, lowered and removed the jack, then stowed it away in Tilly's trunk.

She hugged him, pressed a kiss to his cheek. "You're the best, Henry. Thank you."

"No problem." He squeezed back. "Now go. Enjoy your night."

Tilly waved as she sank into her driver's seat. "Enjoy your kissy time with Bella."

"Hush, you."

Laughing, she closed the door, started up her car, and drove away.

Henry pulled out his cell as he headed to his own car and sent Bella a text.

Finally done. Should I meet you at my place or the diner?

He waited a couple of moments, half-expecting her to text back, but also half-expecting her *not* to. She'd mentioned starting the wedding cakes, and when she was in baking mode, her awareness of her cell phone went by the wayside.

Figuring it would be faster to go to the diner and check if she was, in fact, baking, he started the ignition and headed back into town.

He'd check there first then go to his house.

The drive back into town took less than ten minutes, and one look at the diner through the large plate glass windows at the front of the restaurant told him Bella was still inside. Lights from the kitchen illuminated the round windows of the doors leading down the hall.

He parked on the street, turned off the car, then was moving around the keys on his ring to select the one to the diner's front door when he saw that it wasn't quite closed.

The hairs on the back of his neck prickled.

Pulling out his cell, he used his other hand to tug open the door, wincing when the bell above it twinkled.

Part of him hoped Bella would hear it and come out of the kitchen, and worry tightened his gut into knots when she didn't.

Ridiculous.

She was probably distracted by the cakes.

But the door was unlocked.

That didn't mean anything. Hadn't he just left it open when she'd shown up in town? Darlington was safe—

He reached the doors leading back into the hallway, pushed them open.

And that was the moment he knew his worry wasn't unfounded.

Because silence was the only thing that greeted him.

Not the sound of a mixer or pans rattling. Not Bella's humming as she maneuvered around the space or even the noise of the industrial dishwasher.

He unlocked his phone and dialed Rob as he ran into the kitchen, only realizing that as the call rang that he didn't know what he would tell him. But by the time Rob answered, he knew.

The kitchen was in utter disarray.

A cake pan was overturned on the floor, crumbs of chocolate scattered and squashed into the tiles. The stools lay on their sides, the oven doors open and filling the space with heated air.

"Henry? Are you there?"

The voice in his ear startled him.

His mind was racing, his heart in his throat. He'd almost forgotten he'd been calling Rob.

"This had better not be a booty call butt dial," he grumbled, the words fading, as though he'd brought the phone away from his ear.

"Rob!" Henry said loudly.

"Henry? You there?"

"Yes. I'm at the diner. Something—" His voice broke.

Instantly, Rob's tone went from a mixture of amused and annoyed to alert. "What is it? What happened?"

"Bella." He sucked in a breath. "Sh-she's gone."

RED and blue lights flashed through the front windows of the diner, flickering across the tabletop of the booth Henry sat in.

He dialed Bella's cell again, for the hundredth time in the last hour.

It went straight to voicemail.

Again.

And again.

Fuck. Why hadn't he insisted she come with him?

The officers were in the kitchen, taking pictures, finger-printing the scene while Rob stood near the front door, talking on his cell in a hushed voice that sent Henry's temper prickling.

Why wasn't anyone doing anything?

Why were they all just standing around, twiddling their fucking thumbs when Bella was out there—

He clenched his jaw, forced himself to breathe.

It would do no one any good to run off without a plan.

Clearly, something had gone horribly wrong. Sergio had come back and—

Pam sat down in front of him, notepad open, green eyes holding a hint of sadness. "Are you—" She hesitated.

Henry put down his cell. "What?"

"Are you sure that she didn't just . . . leave—"

He burst to his feet, thrusting his hands into his hair and gripping tightly. *"Are you fucking kidding me?"* he hissed. "You've seen that mess in the kitchen. The overturned food and chairs and—" He swallowed hard, fury in every cell of his body. "And you think that she just up and walked out of here?"

There were fucking drag marks in the doorway, streaks of chocolate smeared into the floor, down the hall.

Pam—fuck that, *Officer Harting*—pushed out of the booth. "I *have* to ask these questions, Henry. We need to have all the information if we're going to find Bella."

"She did not just leave," he growled. "She was testing recipes for the wedding cake she promised to deliver on Saturday. We had plans later tonight to watch a movie. I-I—"

Words failed him.

A hand dropped onto his shoulder, squeezed firmly.

"Steady," Rob said. "We'll find her."

Henry nodded, even though his stomach was churning. "Any word on Sergio?"

He was the most obvious culprit at this point. Who else would want to take Bella? Who else had the most to lose?

No one.

That was who.

And if Henry had wanted to destroy the fucker before . . . well, *now* the need to eviscerate him was the crux on which his every emotion revolved.

Rob shook his head. "Last report had tracked him down to the private airport outside of Salt Lake. Flight plan had been filed for New York, but those can be changed in the air. No credit card records or pings on his passport. For all we know, he's back in New York."

"Or, he could be here."

Rob nodded. "Yes, he could be."

"*Fuck.*"

"It'll be okay," Rob said. "Stay calm and clear-headed. We'll need that."

Henry nodded.

Rob's cell rang and he squeezed Henry's shoulder again before stepping away to answer it.

Pam closed her notebook, stashed it in the pocket of her uniform. "Keep trying her number," she said. "We'll find her."

Except two hours went by.

Then four.

Then eight.

Then twelve.

And there still wasn't a single sign of Bella.

TWENTY

Bella

SHE'D MADE A CRITICAL MISTAKE.

She'd assumed that Sergio had given up on her. That when he'd skipped town after posting bail, he'd realized she wasn't worth the strife and wouldn't come back. She'd thought he wouldn't want to risk getting picked up for the assault charges the District Attorney was planning on filing.

She'd thought she was safe.

What she *hadn't* figured on was her father.

On him showing up in Darlington with his bodyguards and Sergio in tow. She most definitely hadn't anticipated being bundled into the back seat of an SUV or hustled onto his private plane.

And now she was back in Italy.

Staring out at what most would consider a beautiful view—the bright blue waters of the Mediterranean, fishing boats in the distance, colorful buildings surrounding her.

But Bella saw beneath the pretty exterior.

She knew about the concrete wall, the cameras, the guard at her door.

She knew she was trapped.

Sinking down onto the plush chaise lounge, one of the gorgeous pieces of furniture in her expensively furnished prison, Bella stared out the window, trying to figure a way out of her father's house.

No money. No passport. No phone.

Fuck.

She was well and truly fucked.

Her eyes burned with tears, but she refused to let them fall. She hadn't gone back on her own, she'd been forced by a father who had somehow lost his mind. Someone in the house would help her. They *had* to.

But she just couldn't figure out why her father had done it.

Bella was a disappointment, and he never finished a conversation without letting her know that painful truth. He'd threatened to disown her more than once. So why, when she'd finally left for good, had he done this?

Why had he come after her?

She couldn't figure it out. It just—

"None of this makes any sense," she murmured.

A knock at the door had her jumping to her feet, hands braced in front of her. The thick wood panel opened silently, one of her father's bodyguards entering with a garment bag draped over one shoulder.

Bella stepped back, putting the chaise between them.

His name was Raul and he was the one who'd so effectively subdued her at the diner.

She'd barely made it two steps into the hall before he grabbed her, one hand in her hair, the other gripping her wrist and twisting her arm behind her back. He'd had her completely immobilized in under ten seconds.

In the back of the SUV in ten more.

And at the private airfield in less than an hour.

Now Raul dropped the bag onto the bed. "Get dressed."

She shook her head. "No."

His deep brown eyes narrowed. "Get dressed or I'll do it for you."

Part of her felt like she should continue refusing, just on principle. She didn't want to be here. She was desperate to find a way to get out and going along with any of his—and presumably, her father's—orders didn't help her cause.

But one look at his expression warned her that she really didn't want to refuse.

He'd get her in whatever was in that bag and it wouldn't be difficult for him, no matter how big of a fight she put up.

"All right," she said.

"Makeup. Hair. Thirty minutes." He spun around and left the room, and despite the seriousness of her situation, Bella had a hard time not sticking her tongue out at the clipped-out orders.

"Sit. Stay," she muttered, waiting for the door to shut completely before she crossed to the bed. She *would* have locked it behind him, but for obvious reasons, the lock had been removed.

Sighing, she unzipped the bag. A gorgeous navy dress with ruching on the bodice and a lace overlay on the skirt was inside.

No doubt it would be a perfect fit, but it was all Bella could do to not throw the garment out the freaking window. Just the thought of dressing up for her father, for Sergio, for playing the fucking doll all over again turned her stomach.

Or maybe it was the fact that she hadn't eaten for close to twenty-four hours.

She hadn't trusted the food on the plane—her father had kidnapped her already, why would he balk at a simple thing like drugging her into submission. So, she'd refused the food, readying herself to throw a tantrum at customs.

Except *that* opportunity never presented itself.

Her father had stepped off the plane, exchanged some words with an official—and no doubt some bills alongside them —and then they'd been allowed to disembark. Raul had been by her side, the grip on his arm a painful reminder of how easily he could subdue her, and Bella hadn't known whether to show her hand and fight or to go along and try to find a way to escape later.

She should have fought.

Because security at her father's compound had intensified since the last time she'd snuck out.

Before it had felt like protection, safeguards to make sure she wasn't at risk from someone who might try to get to her because of her father's business interests—not that anyone ever seemed to recognize her. She was the floor lamp positioned artistically in the corner of the room, pretty scenery that no one remembered.

But *now*, it was clear the security was in place to keep her there.

How naïve she'd been.

And now she worried she would never see Henry again.

The way Sergio had looked at her on the plane—

Bella shivered. He'd been furious, expression frosty and some dark emotion in his eyes that had her keeping a careful distance from him. She'd embarrassed him again. Not only that, she'd made him look like a deranged fool with a dangerous lack of control, *and* she'd dared to bring charges against him. Then there was the fact that she'd taken up with Henry.

If her father succeeded in marrying her off to him?

She was petrified to consider what he might do to her in retribution.

He'd pushed her down the stairs, had tried to choke her, had chased her, yanking her by the hair. And most of those had been in full view of the public.

Or at least somewhere that they could be easily discovered.

If she were in his home?

Well, Bella thought she wouldn't survive the year.

Because she would keep trying to get out. And keep trying. She would never stop trying to get back to Henry.

Never.

Her eyes drifted back down to the gown in front of her and her sigh was despondent.

Because, for now, she needed to get dressed.

HER HEELS PINCHED like a son of a bitch. The dress was way too tight.

Either she'd gained weight since moving to Darlington or Bella's father was trying to punish her.

She stifled a snort.

Because, one, *of course* he was trying to punish her and, two, she *had* probably gained weight.

All those late-night meals with Henry. All the taste-testing of new desserts she'd planned for the bakery she wanted to open. All the—

Her jaw dropped open as a group of men entered the room.

She'd been shuttled downstairs and into an empty parlor they'd often used for her father's business gatherings. As usual, all the chairs had been removed, replaced by several tall cocktail tables—the kind people stand up to eat at—the sideboard covered with a variety of her father's favorite dishes.

Also as usual, she'd been left standing alone in the space for close to an hour.

Well, alone except for Raul, who was standing near the room's only door.

But that wasn't what made her jaw drop.

"Justin?" she whispered, hope making her heart buoyant.

Aside from dinner at the ranch, she'd only met Kelly's husband a couple of times, but he *had* to recognize her. Or, her heart swelled with hope, maybe they'd found her.

Maybe he'd come to rescue her.

She knew enough about him to understand that his family business was powerful and well-respected.

He could—

But then his eyes connected with hers and her heart sank.

Because he wasn't looking at her with concern or even recognition. No, instead he gave her a faintly appraising once-over, starting at her face and ending at her toes, but other than that, he barely paid her any mind, turning to focus his attention back on whatever her father was saying.

Part of the act.

It had to be.

But . . . what if it wasn't?

What if Justin wanted her family's business more than he wanted to help her? What if—?

No.

Kelly wouldn't have married such a man.

She couldn't have.

But as Bella straightened her shoulders and crossed over to where the men were chatting, she couldn't stop the niggling in her brain that Justin would be able to get her out.

She'd barely reached them when her father shot a glare in her direction. "Wine, Isabella," he snapped. Her hesitation, her moment spent trying to meet Justin's eyes earned her a sharp pinch on her arm. She sucked in a breath, trying and failing to hold back her wince.

"*Now.*"

"I'll help you," Justin said.

Relief coursed through her. He was going to get her out.

He trailed her to the refreshment table, waving off her father's protests. "I'm a guest in your home, it's the least I can do."

Bella grabbed a bottle, positioned herself so her father couldn't see her face.

"Justin," she hissed. "I'm so glad to see you."

He froze, head jerking.

There was something about his eyes . . .

Blinking, she forced herself to focus, to go as slowly as possible as she positioned six glasses and began carefully pouring the red wine made from her father's favorite variety of grapes, Sangiovese.

"I'm . . ." He pressed his lips together, expression bland, as though he were carefully considering what to say. "I'm married."

Bella shook her head. "I know that. Kelly—"

Fingers gripped her wrist, and she nearly dropped the bottle of wine. "What the fuck do you know about Kelly Hamilton?"

Her breath caught and she steadied the bottle. "It's Kelly Roosevelt now," she whispered. "It's me, Justin. Bella. You know I know her and Abbie and the twins. You know *me.* You know I'm Henry's—"

"Isabella!" her father bellowed.

"Coming," she called, grabbing two glasses and hurrying over to give them to him and Sergio before rushing back over to the table and snagging two more.

Justin caught her arm. "Twins?" he asked, hoarsely.

And that was the moment she knew, the moment the pieces aligned in her head and her heart sank to her toes.

"You're not Justin, are you?"

He shook his head, left the sideboard with his glass in hand, rejoining the circle of men.

Bella dropped her gaze to the carpet, blinking back tears as she walked over to distribute the rest of the wine to her father's business associates. Then she strode back to the sideboard, leaning her back against the wall.

Sergio shifted, as though he were going to join her, but her father took him by the back of the neck and whispered something in his ear.

Something that made dark, angry eyes shift in Bella's direction.

Shit.

He listened for a long moment before nodding.

"Food, Isabella," her father ordered in Italian after he'd finished speaking to Sergio. "The others will be here soon, but they can serve themselves."

The men laughed, all except Justin—or the *not* Justin—who probably didn't speak enough Italian to understand the remark.

But *she* got the message loud and clear.

These men were the inner circle.

These men mattered.

And Bella was expected to serve them.

If she didn't—

She shuddered to consider it. Her father had always been demanding, but not like this, not ordering her around in front of the others like she was no better than a servant, and she understood that in her father's eyes, she was worth exactly that much. There was no more slack on her leash, no room for her to go live her own life.

She would do as he wanted, or she would pay the consequences.

He'd find her, no matter where she went, and he'd drag her back here.

She'd never get out.

She would never have the life she'd dreamed of with Henry.

Eyes burning, she began to prepare the six plates, hardly aware of what she was putting on the white porcelain.

"I'm Rex," the not-Justin said, having come back over to refill his glass of wine.

She nodded, moving past him to pile a few shrimp onto her father's plate.

"I'm Justin's twin."

Her breath caught. *Of course*, he was. "Did he—" Hope bubbled up, and she whispered. "Did he send you?"

Silence.

And fuck, hope fizzled like so much smoke.

"No," he finally said.

She nodded, picked up the plate and bringing it to her father, who promptly sent her back to remake it.

"The pastas are touching," he said, as though she were daft and a little marinara mixing with garlic cream sauce was the worst crime she could commit.

But she was reeling and upset, feet screaming, heart aching . . . and so, she remade the plate.

And then again when he said the shrimp were cold.

Never mind that they were *supposed* to be cold.

Finally, she produced a plate he didn't reject, and she worked her way through the others, who all had their various requests.

All except for Rex.

"Henry?" he asked, accepting the plate she thrust at him.

Her eyes shot up, and she nodded.

An eternity passed, several indiscernible emotions crossing his expression, before determination set in. "Trust me," he whispered, and that damn hope bubbled to life again.

But, really, Bella should have known better.

It had been *one* fucking evening and it already felt as though her heart had spent an eternity on a roller coaster. Maybe she had a chance. Maybe she didn't. No, of course she didn't. But maybe—

Rex's fingers brushed the back of her hand. "Just trust me."

Except, he didn't do anything to warrant that trust.

Instead, Rex ignored her the rest of the evening, demanding more plates of food and eating like a glutton as the rest of the men—the lower circle of her father's associates—joined the party. And that said nothing of how much he drank.

He kept refilling his glass. Over and over. Until Raul had to sling his arm around Rex's shoulders and escort him from the room.

Until Bella was alone, all over again.

Rex Roosevelt was just like the rest of them.

SHE'D JUST HUNG the dress back up in her closet when she heard a noise that sent the hairs on her nape prickling and her movements into high gear.

Someone was breaking in.

Or rather, someone had let themselves into her room since her door didn't have a lock.

She'd shoved a chair in front of it, for all the good that did her in this moment. The screech of its feet sliding against the tile floor was what Bella had heard.

Hurrying, she threw on the first clothes she could reach—sweats, a T-shirt, even bare feet into sneakers. Both because she didn't want to be in just her underwear if it was Sergio who'd come in and also because she wanted to have the chance to run if the opportunity presented itself.

Then she searched for a weapon.

The fancy suite she was being kept in had a designer wardrobe and makeup filled drawers, silk sheets, and plush rugs. A luxurious prison, to be sure, but not one exactly rife with weapons.

In the end, footsteps prompted her to grab the first thing she saw.

A curling iron.

She darted into the bathroom and snatched it up then hid behind the partially open door.

"Isabella?" came a hushed male voice. The footsteps drifted closer.

She clenched the plastic handle tightly, lifted it above her head.

A shadow crossed the threshold of the bathroom then a leg . . . a torso.

Bella closed her eyes and swung.

Thunk.

"Fuck!" the voice said, stepping fully into the bathroom and wincing as he rubbed the top of his head.

She froze. "But you're drunk." A whisper.

Rex's mouth curved. "Either that or I'm really good at pretending I am."

"I saw you drink those bottles of wine." Two of them. By himself.

"I drank a few glasses," he admitted. "But your father's fern drank more. I probably killed it"—a shrug—"though I don't think that'll bother you much."

Bella smiled. "Not at all actually."

"Good," Rex said. "So, you want to get out of here?"

She laughed at the casual tone he used, like they were getting ready to leave a restaurant or a boring party.

"Yes," she said. "I'd like to go home. But what about the guards?"

"I was busy while I was passed out drunk in my room. I called in some help and"—he held up a bag—"I found your passport."

Hope bubbled up in her. "But—"

He took her arm. "There's too much to explain now. We need to be in position in ten minutes. Can you trust me to get you out?"

She looked into his eyes, saw earnestness but also the barest hint of a shadow, as though he expected her to say no.

But, fuck, what choice to Bella have?

Stay and—

She shuddered to think of it.

Or trust Justin's brother and hope that he kept up his end of the bargain.

A nod. The decision not one that took long to ponder. She wanted to get home to Darlington, to Henry.

She'd do whatever it took.

"Get me out of here, Rex."

TWENTY-ONE

Henry

HE WAS SITTING in the kitchen of Roosevelt Ranch when Justin's phone rang.

Two days without a word from Bella, forty-eight hours with no sightings of her or Sergio, but still Henry's heart leaped at the vibration.

Maybe—

Justin shook his head slightly. "Just Rex."

Once Henry would have thought Rex to be pretty much the worst kind of scum out there, but now he knew differently. Rex was an asshole, but he was on a completely different scale than Sergio.

Justin rejected the call, slid it back into his pocket. "How are you—" He broke off with a sigh and pulled his cell back out. "Let me get this. Otherwise, he'll just keep calling." He swiped, put the phone up to his ear. "Listen, Rex. This isn't a good —*what?*"

Henry straightened at the shocked tone but then rolled his eyes.

The bastard had probably made another shitty business decision. Or knocked up—

"Okay," Justin said. "Okay, I'll—*we'll* be there in . . . *fuck*, I don't know. As soon as we can." He hung up. "Let's go. It's Bella. I'll explain on the way."

"I—" Shock had Henry in its grip for one long moment, but then Justin rushed for the front door and the action sprung Henry into motion.

They ran to the garage, bypassing the wedding, but spending precious minutes navigating around all the cars before they managed to make their way to the main road. All the while, Henry's head was spinning, wanting to demand information, but knowing he needed to wait until, at the very least, they maneuvered past the reveling guests.

The moment they were clear, Justin dialed Rob and put him on speakerphone.

"I just got a call from Rex," Justin said. "He's on the private plane and will be landing at the airfield in less than an hour." His eyes shot to Henry's, and he said the unbelievable words Henry had been hoping for since Justin had mentioned her name. Impossible, because how could Rex have anything to do with Bella, but still wishing for them all the same.

"Rex says Bella is with him. Apparently, he met her father in Italy, they were going to do business, but then Bella was there and—" Justin shook his head. "Well, that's all he would say. That she's fine and next to him, and they're landing at the airport in just under an hour."

To Rob's credit, he regained himself faster than Henry.

"Holy shit." Then a deep breath rattled through the airwaves. "Okay, I'll get on the horn and see who's closest so they can meet the plane and make sure she's safe. How long until you guys are there?"

"Depending on how fast I drive," Justin replied, "hour and a half?"

"Me, too," Rob said. "Drive fast. I'll clear your way."

He hung up, and Henry turned to Justin.

"Do you think Rex—" He cut off the question, not wanting to voice the possibility that Bella might not actually be on the plane.

"No," Justin said quietly. "She's there."

And then he floored it, making the drive in less time than Henry could have imagined, but it was still the longest hour and a half of his life.

Finally, *finally,* they pulled into the private airfield parking lot. A jet was parked there, the only large plane amongst the single engines. Its doors were open, the stairs extended.

Henry waited just long enough for Justin to put the car into park before popping his door and sprinting up the stairs.

He didn't breathe until he saw her.

Curled up on a leather couch, blanket pulled up to her chin.

"She's just sleeping. Couldn't hold out any longer."

Henry turned and saw Justin's twin standing near the cockpit. Officer Harting stood next to him. He hadn't registered them, hadn't seen anything aside from Bella.

"Is she—"

"She's okay. Just exhausted. We didn't have the easiest time getting out of Italy."

Henry nodded, figuring that was enough for now.

Later, they would have the whole story.

Right now, he was taking her home.

He crossed over to Bella, scooped her up into his arms, and carried her down the stairs. Justin was there, opening the back door, helping him maneuver her inside. A few minutes later, they were on the road again.

Rob flew past them in a cruiser, and a few seconds later Justin's phone rang.

He answered with the volume low, though Bella hadn't stirred.

"You got her?"

"Yes," Justin said. "I can't take her back to my house. Henry's?"

"Yup. I'll get a car there. I'm going to speak to Rex and then I'll head to Henry's place."

"Should I make some calls?"

Henry had managed to get a seat belt around Bella's waist and still hold her, cradling her against the bumps, but he was following the conversation, still understood what Justin was alluding to.

Kelly's husband had spent many years in the military, and he knew some very powerful folks in private security.

Henry was all-in for whatever they could do to ensure Bella's safety. He'd sell the diner, move out of state, change his name, find a way to finance bodyguards—

Anything, so long as she never had to go through this again.

Anything so he didn't have to spend another sleepless night petrified that she was hurting and scared . . . or worse.

Rob cleared his throat. "Will they stop that asshole from coming after her again?"

"They have ways of making sure that doesn't happen again."

"Then probably," Rob said. "But wait until I talk to Rex first. This is way the fuck out my jurisdiction, but I want to make sure we have all the information we need to keep Bella safe." A pause. "Once that's done, I'll call my contact at the FBI, and he can advise the department from there."

"Henry?" Justin asked.

He nodded, eyes locked on Bella, memorizing every detail,

promising himself he would never take another moment with her for granted.

"He's with us," Justin translated for him to Rob and then hung up.

They'd driven another fifteen minutes, the sun firmly behind the hills, the sky an ever-deepening navy, when Bella finally stirred.

Her head rolled from side to side, she stretched, and then went ramrod straight.

She jerked, eyes flashing open, mouth parting as though to scream.

Then she saw Henry.

And burst into tears.

Huge gasping sobs that absolutely broke his heart. "It's okay," he told her, repeating the words over and over again. "You're safe now. I'm here."

Her arms wrapped around his neck and she crawled into his lap, tears soaking into his shirt. "I thought—" Her breath caught. "I thought—" But she couldn't finish the sentence.

"I know," he murmured. "I know, sweetheart. You're home now. You're safe." He whispered the mantra over and over again, until finally her spine softened, her breathing slowed.

Finally she nodded, as though hearing the words for the first time and burrowed into him.

"Sleep now," he said. "I've got you."

LATER THAT NIGHT, Bella woke with a start, lurching against him, panicked for long, heartbreaking moments until his voice finally penetrated.

Henry held it together until she fell back to sleep, the terror of the last few days clearly taking its toll on her. He slipped out of bed and moved quietly into the bathroom.

There he opened the medicine cabinet, pulled out the little black box hidden on the top shelf.

Above Bella's sight. So she couldn't stumble on it.

Henry had bought it five years before.

Had planned on giving it to her then, had intended to give it to her only a few days ago.

And now?

Henry shoved it back on the shelf.

How could he?

He stared at himself in the mirror, wondering all over again why he'd left Bella alone.

He should have known.

Yet, how *could* he have known?

But dammit, he fucking hadn't protected her five years ago, and he hadn't protected her now. He was fucking useless and—

The door slid open on a quiet squeak, Bella's eyes peering at him through the gap.

She hesitated, and he put out a hand. "Come here, sweetheart."

Then she was in his arms. The guilt abated, for the moment, anyway, because the relief that they'd somehow found their way back to each other was so great.

"Every time I close my eyes, I keep thinking of them. I keep worrying they'll—"

She clamped her mouth closed, biting back the rest of her words.

Henry cupped her cheek and tilted her head back so he could see her face. Dark circles still ringed the skin beneath her eyes, and she was very pale. But she was alive and in his arms. That was enough for now.

"I know, baby. But it was traumatic. You have to give yourself time to heal."

They'd talked to Rex, now knew that it wasn't just Sergio who'd kidnapped Bella, that her father had an equal, or worse, hand in it.

"I don't want time to heal!" she snapped, pushing out of his embrace and pacing away. "I'm so tired of my father trying to ruin my life. I'm so tired of being a pawn that he doesn't want and yet can't let go. He absolutely despises me, but because I chose to leave, he had to punish me."

He watched her stride across the bathroom, back and forth, back and forth. The fire in her eyes, the first sign he'd seen since her return, settled the gaping wound in his heart.

Oh, it was still there, would probably never completely go away, same as the wound from his dad, but the guilt and worry weren't so all-encompassing.

He could finally breathe, could focus on being what Bella needed.

"I know."

"He hates me." She shook her head. "I don't know why he wants to control me. Why can't he just let me go? Forget I existed."

"Men like him can never let it go, not when they feel like they've been bested."

She swallowed hard. "I know. That's why I'm so worried about Rex. He took a huge risk in helping me. I don't even know how many people he paid off—officials, security guards."

"Rex will be okay," he assured her. "He can afford to hire security."

"But—"

"And there's also the fact that Justin's friends visited your father and Sergio."

Bella frowned. "Why would it matter if Justin's friends visited?"

"Because he has some friends in very high places. Friends that can make you disappear without a trace, but also friends that can make your father's business prospects dry up." Henry shrugged. "Justin just told me they found evidence of your father participating in some unsavory, and decidedly illegal activities. If he or Sergio or one of their lackeys gets within even a hundred miles of you, that information will be passed along to the proper authorities."

"Oh."

He smiled for what felt like the first time in a century. "Yeah, oh."

"And we'll keep some security around for a while. Install a system here and at the diner, have some guys keep watch on the house until you're comfortable."

Bella laced her fingers with his. "So, if you've done all that, then why are you in here beating yourself up?"

Henry froze. "I'm—"

"Don't deny it." She tugged him into the bedroom and over to the bed. "I know you, love. I know you're beating yourself up because you have some notion that you should have protected me."

He shook his head. "I shouldn't have—"

"Don't." She lay down, coaxed him to cuddle up next to her. "Don't say you shouldn't have helped Tilly. I love this town. I love the way everyone looks after one another." She rested her head on his shoulder. "I love you."

"I love you, too."

"Hold me while I sleep?"

"Always."

Her voice, when it came a few minutes later, was gentle. "I know you're going to feel guilty for a long time. Because you're a

good man and because you care about me, but you need to come
to terms with the fact that this wasn't your fault."

"I—"

"No," she said, firmer now. "No. You don't get to shoulder
this. My father and Sergio were at fault. Not you."

"Sweetheart—"

She sat up then glared down at him. "Do you blame *me* for
being kidnapped?"

"Fuck no," he growled.

"Then you can't blame yourself, either."

He opened his mouth, found it covered with her hand.

"I know it will take you time to believe it, so I'm going to be
patient." One half of her mouth curved. "For the moment."

He touched her cheek. "I love you."

A full smile now. "And I love you, but you want to be here
for me? I need you to be present, not sneaking off to mentally
berate yourself. I need us to live the future I dreamed of for five
years." She turned her head, pressed a kiss to his palm. "I need
the diner and a bakery. I need you in my bed every night. I need
babies and puppies. And I"—she pressed her mouth to his
—"need you."

"You have me." A kiss to her forehead, each cheek, her nose.
"Forever."

"I can deal with that."

And then as they drifted off to sleep, the sound of their
laughter echoing in the air around them, Henry thought that he
might just be able to give her that ring after all.

TWENTY-TWO

Bella

SHE'D FINALLY COMPLETED a wedding cake.

Or nearly, she thought, adding one last flower to the grouping of red and white blooms cascading down the side of the cake.

"That's beautiful," Melissa said.

Bella bumped her shoulder against her friend's. "I think you're just glad that I didn't get out of making the cake this time."

Melissa's eyes twinkled. "Oh, definitely. Kidnapping as a way to get out of commitments, totally solid plan."

"Takes one to know one."

They fist-bumped and giggled.

It was a relief to be able to laugh with someone about what happened, but also to be able to talk with someone who knew what it was like to go through something so traumatic. Melissa had passed along the name of the therapist she'd spoken to after her own harrowing abduction, a much-appreciated gesture.

Bella knew she would need to eventually talk with someone, but she wanted a little more time to get her legs back under her.

Only six weeks had passed since Rex delivered her safely back to Darlington and while she still had the occasional nightmare, they were coming less frequently. It also helped that Justin's *friends* delivered weekly reports on her father and Sergio's whereabouts. Not the healthiest thing ever, but she took a lot of comfort in knowing where they were . . . though in reality, she didn't give a damn where they were, so long as that was far, *far* away from her.

More importantly, she'd seen Henry relax over the last weeks, going from not being able to stand having her out of his sight, to leaving her alone for hours at a time.

Like today.

Though, she was surrounded by people.

And he'd texted a half-dozen times.

Still, it was progress and she was just happy Henry had managed to put the majority of his guilt behind him.

She'd officially moved her stuff out of the apartment and into his house and was looking for a commercial space to open the bakery, but for now, she continued to take shifts at the diner when she could.

Because the majority of the time was spent filling its cold cases with baked goods that the people of Darlington snatched up in rapid succession.

They'd even written an article in the local newspaper accusing her of making everyone in town fat.

Outwardly, she suggested a 5K to raise money for P.E. programs at the local elementary, middle, and high schools, but internally she'd been thrilled to have her very own news story in the *Darlington Gazette*.

Finally, she'd made it.

But, celebrity status or not, it was time to get this cake out to the venue.

"Ready?" she asked, nudging one more flower into the arrangement. Melissa was going to help her carry it from the small kitchen where she'd put on the finishing touches, out to the cake table in the pavilion.

And it was going to be filmed for the show.

Bella sent up a mental prayer. Please let her not ruin another wedding cake.

"Ready," Melissa chirped, grabbing the other side of the stand. They lifted on three and carefully navigated the space, not breathing until it was safely on the table.

Bella stepped back, wiped her forehead on a towel. "Damn. I did good."

Melissa snorted, but she was smiling. "Hell, yes, you did." A beat. "You now know this will never end, right? You'll be baking Darlington's wedding cakes for all eternity."

Bella grinned over at her. "I can live with that."

Her phone buzzed in her pocket, and she pulled it out to see another text from Henry.

Melissa rolled her eyes. "That man needs to chill."

Bella hardly heard her because the text wasn't checking up on her. Instead, it said:

Our place. Sunset?

She grinned.

I'll be there.

Another buzz.

Will you bring me cake?

But before she could type out a response, he had her bursting out into laughter at a GIF he sent of a puppy with a surprisingly innocent face surrounded by the evidence of his decidedly *not* innocent playtime with a roll of toilet paper.

Funny you ask because I might have made an extra pan.

Her cell vibrated.

I'll bring the forks.

"Okay," Melissa said, "I take it back. The man is good. Too good."

Bella happened to agree and loved him all the more for it. "I think I'm going to take off. Can you—?"

Melissa made a shooing movement. "Get out of here before you miss the sunset."

Bella grinned and waved, stopping only to pick up the smaller cake she'd made for Henry. Then she drove to his spot and carried it up to where he waited at the top of the hill, two forks in hand.

She knew what it cost him to not hover, to give her the space to go about her life without a babysitter when part of him was still always on edge about her safety.

"How'd you get here?" She'd only just gotten her license and had borrowed his car to drop off the cake.

He slid an arm around her waist. "Justin," he said and nudged her down to their rock. She was shocked to see he'd gone through the trouble of laying out a blanket and basket. There was even a candle in the center. "Not the most practical place for a picnic," he told her, pulling the cake from her hands and setting it on top before lifting her up. "But I couldn't resist."

Practical or not, it was both beautiful *and* sweet.

"Please, tell me there's Cobb salad in that basket."

Henry smirked. "We need *something* to counter all the sugar you keep forcing me to eat."

A snort. "Forcing. Ha." But she'd already opened the basket and was digging out a container of her favorite salad. "Oh, thank you. I'm starving." She scooped up a giant bite, shoved it in her mouth—

He lifted a hand. "Wait—"

Crunch.

She winced. *He* winced.

"I was going to . . ."

Bella lifted a napkin to her mouth, deposited the object that had nearly cracked her tooth inside of it.

"I figured you'd see it in the slice of egg."

She stared down at the ring, a simple band with a diamond in its center. "I didn't," she whispered.

"Bella." Her eyes met his. "I wished for this five years ago. And I know it's fast and so much has happened in so short a time now. But what I've learned from my dad, from you, from *us* is that we have to grab on to our chances for happiness with two hands." He swallowed. "Will you marry me? It doesn't have to be today or even this year but—"

"Shut up." Bella laughed at the expression on his face as she wiped the ring clean. "I love you. Of course, I'll marry you. Today, tomorrow, or next year. I just want a life with you, Henry Miller, however we end up making it work." A beat. "Now, put this damned ring on my finger and kiss me."

And for once, he didn't tease her or argue or delay.

He slid the ring on and kissed her until they missed the sunset all together and the sky was dark.

Then he kissed her again as the stars shone brightly in the sky.

EPILOGUE

Rex

HE DROVE down the dark road, trying to figure out why he was still in Darlington, Utah almost two months after he'd deposited Bella back with her one true love, Henry.

Barf.

Love was for idiots.

Or pussies.

Or people who were insanely, sickeningly happy.

Ugh.

Rex was jealous. He knew it. He embraced it.

But that didn't change the fact he wasn't the kind of person who fell in love. Or rather, he didn't *allow* himself to fall in love. He'd seen the way his father had loved his mother—a touching Hollywood scene if there ever was one, filled with so much devotion and affection that when she'd died, he'd changed.

Part of him had died, too.

And so Rex and Justin had lost *both* parents.

That was the troubling part of so-called happily ever afters.

They never lasted.

Rex sighed because the real casualties in those failed or aborted happy endings were the kids. *They* suffered. *They* lost it all. *They*—

"Fuck!" he said and swerved, almost clipping the car pulled barely on the shoulder.

No hazard lights flashing. No flares. Nothing but a dark shape silhouetted against the moonlight. Were they trying to get themselves killed?

He slowed and turned around, heading back to the parked car.

His tirade about responsibility was on the tip of his tongue and—*ha*—if anyone even knew that *he'd* thought the word responsibility, they would have keeled over and dropped dead.

Responsibility and Rex Roosevelt did not belong in the same sentence.

He was the screw-up.

He was the bad guy.

He was pulling over behind the car.

Rex parked behind them and turned on his hazard lights before getting out. He'd extended a hand to knock when he saw the woman inside. Spot-lit by his car's headlights, she looked like an angel with pale blonde hair and delicate features.

Or at least from the glimpse he caught, they *seemed* delicate.

He only caught hints of a pert nose, plump lips, and a petite chin because she was spending a lot of time banging her face against the steering wheel.

Rex hesitated and almost turned away, leaving her to whatever sort of mental breakdown she was determined to have, but just as he'd taken a step back toward his car, his conscience pinged.

The annoying bastard had been all too busy lately.

He sighed but knew he couldn't leave her, and so he blew out a breath, raised his hand, and knocked on the window.

The woman inside jumped.

Her gaze shot to his for one long moment before her eyes slid closed, head dropping down to the steering wheel.

But Rex barely noticed.

Because one look from *her,* and he'd felt like he'd been struck over the head by a two-by-four.

Or maybe hit in the ass by Cupid's arrow.

She was . . . different . . . wonderful . . .

And he wanted her.

—Desire at Roosevelt Ranch coming November 17th

ROOSEVELT RANCH SERIES

Did you miss any of the other Roosevelt Ranch books? Check out excerpts from the series below or find the full series here: amazon.com/gp/product/B07Q8VRK9Y

***

DISASTER AT ROOSEVELT RANCH
Book One
(books2read.com/DARR)

I had never thought of a plus sign as a bad thing.

Of course, I'd never had one show up on a stick I'd peed on. Kudos to me, that changed today.

My knees wobbled, and the idiotic white piece of plastic rattled as I set it on the scarred Formica countertop.

Brown eyes—mine—stared back at me accusingly in the mirror. "You've done it now."

A baby.

My hand found my stomach. Still flat, still the same.

Even though so much had changed.

The bathroom door rattled as a fist slammed against the thin plank of wood. "Move it, Kel! Food's up and your tables are restless."

"Coming!" I called as I wrapped the test in a paper towel before shoving it deep into my purse.

I couldn't leave it here. Not where anyone—where *Henry*—might see it. He would get his back up, storm out to the ranch where he-who-must-not-be-named lived, and drag the no-good, low down piece of crap into town for a proper whooping.

And I might just want to let him.

With a sigh, I washed my hands and left the bathroom.

It was my own fault. I knew the type of man Rex was.

I'd fallen into his bed anyway.

"Regret never fails to burn like a mother," I muttered as I swept into the kitchen, grabbed the plates from the pass, and started hustling toward my table.

"What was that?" Henry asked as he flipped a burger.

"Nothing." I hefted the tray filled with six plates and various food accessories—ketchup, extra dressing, and napkins— with practiced ease.

Oh, God. I was going to be huge and pregnant and . . . waiting tables.

Good luck to the customers, because I lacked the sincerity and cheerfulness that seemed to come naturally to most wait- resses on a normal day. I could only imagine what was going to happen when my hormones raged.

Using my back, I pushed through the swinging door and promptly stumbled to a stop.

He was here. *Rex* was here.

Stupidly, my heart raced. He'd changed his mind. He'd—

The man's eyes flicked to mine, completely unrecognizing and indifferent. My momentary burst of hope disintegrated.

He was going to pretend not to know me? To not *recognize* me?

The jerk! The rotten—

Except . . . there was something off about him. I squinted, trying to discern the change, but the tray was taking its toll on my arms. I tore my gaze away from Rex to practically hurl the dishes at my customers.

"Anything else?" I asked, and was thankful when there weren't any requests.

Two seconds later, I was in front of Rex.

Who wasn't *actually* Rex.

Oh, he was the right height and had the same square jaw

and the same gorgeous, sun-kissed skin, but *this* man wasn't the one I'd slept with.

"Hi," he said, his green eyes warm. They were a brilliant emerald and just as inviting as they'd been in the picture I'd seen on Rex's desk. "Can I just sit anywhere?"

My nod was jerky. "I'll get you a menu."

Fingers brushed my arm—calloused fingers that felt both familiar and different.

"You okay?"

I forced a smile, my stomach churning. This could *not* be happening. "Just perfect—"

And that was the moment I puked all over Rex's twin's shoes.

—Get your copy books2read.com/DARR.

HEARTBREAK AT ROOSEVELT RANCH
Book Two
(books2read.com/HARR)

I straightened from putting the last plate into the dishwasher and stretched for a towel to wipe my hands. I was exhausted after twenty-four straight hours with the kids, and Rob still wasn't home. Not to mention, I needed to make cupcakes for Max's school—and somehow do it without sugar.

So the ensuing crash upstairs was not welcome.

Dropping the towel, I whisper-sprinted up to the second floor—running on tiptoes while hopping, leaping, and skipping over every toy obstacle, creaky floorboard, and rogue crayon along the way.

The light was on in Max's room, and considering that I had

made this trek a half dozen times in the last hour, I was out of patience.

"You need to go to sleep," I growled, throwing open the door, my fierce mom glare already in place.

Except the devil child *was* asleep.

He'd fallen out of bed, crashed onto an entire village of Legos—scattering them to hell and back—and was dead asleep.

My heart gave a little squeeze even as the logical part of me recognized the giant mess I'd be picking up tomorrow.

It was just that face.

A cupid's bow of bright pink lips, slightly parted, rosy cheeks, and mussed hair. The boy was cute, and it was hard to believe he was part of me, that he'd come from my body.

I clucked my tongue at myself, knowing I was being ridiculous and romantic and *Melissa-like* because I'd spent the day with Kelly and her toddler, Abby.

My baby sister had a baby. And a man. And was all grown up—

Oh God. There I went with the tears again.

Swiping a finger under each eye, I navigated the minefield of toys as I made my way over to Max. I gave an internal grunt as I lifted the little—or not so little, anymore—monkey and tucked him back into bed.

One hastily constructed barrier of pillows and blankets and stuffed Minecraft toys later, and I was heading back out of the room.

I flicked the light off, started to leave—

"Too dark, Mommy," he murmured.

A sigh. Back on it went. "Good night, sweetheart."

"Night."

This time I made it to the top of the stairs before a sound stopped me.

It wasn't the kids. No. This was more like . . . buzzing?

I cocked my head and listened, then made my way to my bedroom, a growing pile of toys in my arms as I went.

The door was open, and I walked inside, dumping the pile on the coverlet before stopping to pinpoint the sound.

I felt my pockets for my cell. Not even two days before, I'd scoured the house for my phone, it somehow having fallen out of my pocket, ending up under the dresser. It had taken darn near fifty calls and a search of the entire house before I'd found it.

Those locating apps were all well and good, but they couldn't tell a person which room in a house their phone was. Which meant the app, for my day-to-day exploits, was pretty much useless.

I hardly left home at all except for the kids' activities and school pickup or drop off.

Or if Rob needed something down at the station.

And that was fine. My place was at home. The kids needed me, Rob needed me. It was just that sometimes . . .

No. Don't get sidetracked.

My phone *was* in my pocket. The sound wasn't coming from beneath the dresser.

It was coming from the bed.

I peered under, saw nothing, and I was reaching for Rob's flashlight in his nightstand when I realized where exactly the noise was originating from.

My hand slid between the mattress and box spring, jumping a little when the object buzzed against my fingers.

"What—?" I pulled it out, saw it was an older-looking iPhone. Why was there—

Then I saw the texts. An entire screen worth of them.

And my heart froze solid.

I'm heading to the hotel.

Where are you?

Don't keep me waiting, honey.

I need you.

The question wasn't why Rob had hidden a phone under his side of the mattress. It was why someone named Celeste was calling him honey and telling *my* husband that she needed him.

Downstairs, I heard the garage door rumble open and close, the clink of Rob's keys on the kitchen counter. "Miss?" he called softly up the stairs.

My voice was gone, my throat tight. My eyes burned, and still, I held the phone. It wasn't until I heard him walking down the hall to the bedroom that I sprang into motion.

I shoved the phone back under the mattress and scooped up the toys.

Rob stopped short in the doorway. "Oh." He smiled. "I called you."

"Sorry, I was cleaning."

He touched my cheek, slid past me. "You don't have to do that."

"It's my job," I said brightly, and if it was too bright then what did it matter anyway?

My husband was moving toward the bathroom, already unbuttoning his shirt. "Is there a plate for me?"

I turned, saw he'd paused, and forced a smile. "Yup. I'll heat it up for you."

"Thanks, love."

"Of course." I walked out of the bedroom but didn't go downstairs.

Instead, I hesitated in the hall, silent and waiting.

And my gut tied itself into knots when I heard Rob's footfalls across the carpet, the slide of his hand beneath the mattress as he pulled out the phone.

—Get your copy at books2read.com/HARR.

COLLISION AT ROOSEVELT RANCH
Book Three
(books2read.com/CARR)

Haley

"Just play already," Haley muttered, fumbling with her phone. She'd stopped at an intersection on her way home from the hospital, and she just wanted to boy band love, okay?

Exhaustion tugged at her brain, her eyes burned, and her shoulders ached. She was also very close to tears.

She'd lost a patient that night.

It hadn't been her fault. It hadn't been anyone's fault. Sometimes those things just happened—accidents, everyone working frantically to pull someone back from the brink, a body failing—but that didn't make losing a patient any easier.

Her job was to save them.

Life was such a fragile thing. As a nurse, she knew that firsthand. But she'd also left her job at the busy county hospital in California and returned home to Darlington, Utah because she was tired of seeing people die every day.

Haley was damned good at compartmentalizing, but sometimes things weren't so easy to shove down.

Sometimes those fuckers kept popping back up.

Sometimes the cases hit too close to home—

A horn beeped behind her and she jumped. "Shit." Her phone still not cooperating, the poppy upbeat notes of her favorite boy bands remained silently trapped inside the techno-logical device that never seemed to work correctly.

Even though it was brand spanking new.

Even though she'd gotten a complete tutorial from her brother-in-law, who had gone through all the troubleshooting with her.

Even though the freaking tech from the phone store had personally tested the Bluetooth by coming out to her car and showing her how it worked.

Technology. She repelled it.

Or rather, she was technology's kryptonite.

Two minutes around her, and she destroyed even the most powerful device.

"Yay me," she murmured, dropping the phone to her passen-ger's seat. Haley shouldn't be fussing with it anyway, not while she was driving, but—*a sigh*—she'd really wanted to escape for the rest of her drive.

Not to be.

Checking for traffic, she pulled carefully through the inter-section. Darlington was a small town, and signals were few and far between, but the roads at this time of the night were dark . . . and she'd had a deer jump right in front of her car once before.

The car that had honked at her turned to follow her down the bumpy lane, headlights very bright in her rearview mirror, the front bumper just inside that bubble all drivers had.

This one triggered her slightly-too-close alert but not the this-fucker-better-back-off alarm.

Her lips curved.

So, she might have gotten used to the more aggressive drivers of Northern California.

The thought of her first months in San Francisco, of the busy roads, the huge buildings, the patient care that both chal-lenged and devastated her, brought a smile to her face. For all the reasons she'd come home, Haley was still happy she'd left Utah.

Small town life was . . . well, small.

Or it had seemed that way before she'd left.

Now she saw how much her world had expanded by being . . . well, herself. Having *found* herself, as cliché as that sounded.

She'd left a little girl, never feeling like she could measure up, and had returned—

Still feeling like she would never live up to her expectations. *Ha*. That was life for a girl. But Haley had come back with the understanding that *she* was the one setting impossible standards. Progress, yes? And she was a work in progress.

Step one was realizing that not everything she did had to be perfect and exacting.

Which was all well and good for her Pinterest attempts —*cough*—fails.

It didn't work as well for her patients.

Hence the mental punch fest happening in her brain alongside the driving need for cheesy pop music to provide her with some escapism.

Had she done everything right? What had she missed? What could she have done differently? Would any of it had made any difference?

No.

No, it wouldn't have.

Tears stung her eyes, and she blinked them away.

If Haley hadn't blinked at that moment, things might not have turned out as they did.

But she *did* blink, right as two other things happened simultaneously.

Music exploded through her speakers—the Backstreet Boys singing about the way they wanted it—and a deer jumped into the road.

By the time her lids had flashed back open, the jar of pop-tastic noise accelerating the process to near inhuman speed, the flipping deer was directly in front of her bumper and *definitely* within her bubble.

Frankly, it was firmly in the she-was-gonna-plow-it-down-and-make-a-deer-pancake zone.

"Fuck!" She slammed on her brakes.

Tires screeched. She braced for impact and then . . .

The deer executed a leap that was fitting of a figure skater and jumped clear of her car.

Haley sighed in relief. For a single heartbeat.

Because that relief disappeared before the next.

Her body was propelled forward as the driver who had been —and here came that damned bubble analogy again—following her too closely before, plowed into her from behind.

And she didn't even have time to snort about the dirtiness of that particular innuendo before the seatbelt yanked tightly across her chest. Pain shot up her leg as her foot compressed more firmly on the brake pedal, but before she could focus too much on the sensation, her head smacked against the top of the steering wheel.

"Fucking bubbles," she slurred as everything went black.

—Get your copy at books2read.com/CARR

DESIRE AT ROOSEVELT RANCH
Book Five
(books2read.com/DesireARR)

Rex

He drove down the dark road, trying to figure out why he was still in Darlington, Utah almost two months after he'd deposited Bella back with her one true love, Henry.

Barf.

Love was for idiots.

Or pussies.

Or people who were insanely, sickeningly happy.

Ugh.

Rex was jealous. He knew it. He embraced it.

But that didn't change the fact he wasn't the kind of person who fell in love. Or rather, he didn't *allow* himself to fall in love. He'd seen the way his father had loved his mother—a touching Hollywood scene if there ever was one, filled with so much devotion and affection that when she'd died, he'd changed.

Part of him had died, too.

And so Rex and Justin had lost *both* parents.

That was the troubling part of so-called happily ever afters.

They never lasted.

Rex sighed because the real casualties in those failed or aborted happy endings were the kids. *They* suffered. *They* lost it all. *They*—

"Fuck!" he said and swerved, almost clipping the car pulled barely on the shoulder.

No hazard lights flashing. No flares. Nothing but a dark shape silhouetted against the moonlight. Were they trying to get themselves killed?

He slowed and turned around, heading back to the parked car.

His tirade about responsibility was on the tip of his tongue and—*ha*—if anyone even knew that *he'd* thought the word responsibility, they would have keeled over and dropped dead.

Responsibility and Rex Roosevelt did not belong in the same sentence.

He was the screw-up.

He was the bad guy.

He was pulling over behind the car.

Rex parked behind them and turned on his hazard lights before getting out. He'd extended a hand to knock when he saw the woman inside. Spot-lit by his car's headlights, she looked like an angel with pale blonde hair and delicate features.

Or at least from the glimpse he caught, they *seemed* delicate.

He only caught hints of a pert nose, plump lips, and a petite chin because she was spending a lot of time banging her face against the steering wheel.

Rex hesitated and almost turned away, leaving her to whatever sort of mental breakdown she was determined to have, but just as he'd taken a step back toward his car, his conscience pinged.

The annoying bastard had been all too busy lately.

He sighed but knew he couldn't leave her, and so he blew out a breath, raised his hand, and knocked on the window.

The woman inside jumped.

Her gaze shot to his for one long moment before her eyes slid closed, head dropping down to the steering wheel.

But Rex barely noticed.

Because one look from *her,* and he'd felt like he'd been struck over the head by a two-by-four.

Or maybe hit in the ass by Cupid's arrow.

She was . . . different . . . wonderful . . .

And he wanted her.

—Desire at Roosevelt Ranch coming November 17th

ACKNOWLEDGMENTS

Thank you to Christine, Kay, and Julie for helping me shape my thoughts into something readable! I couldn't do it without you. And the biggest thanks to you, my readers. Thank you so much for supporting my books and these stories that fill up my brain. I love to hear from you guys! You can connect with me via my newsletter (http://eepurl.com/bdnmEj), my website (elise-faber.com), my Facebook group (facebook.com/groups/fabinators), or you can reach me via email at elisefaberauthor@gmail.com.

Love you guys!
—XOXO,
E

ALSO BY ELISE FABER

(SEE A FULL LISTING AND DESCRIPTIONS AT
WWW.ELISEFABER.COM/ALL-BOOKS)

Roosevelt Ranch Series (all stand alone)

Disaster at Roosevelt Ranch

Heartbreak at Roosevelt Ranch

Collision at Roosevelt Ranch

Regret at Roosevelt Ranch

Desire at Roosevelt Ranch (November 17th)

Billionaire's Club (all stand alone)

Bad Night Stand

Bad Breakup

Bad Husband

Bad Hookup

Bad Divorce

Bad Boyfriend (Oct 6th, 2019)

Gold Hockey (all stand alone)

Blocked

Backhand

Boarding

Benched

Breakaway

Breakout (Dec 15th, 2019)

ABOUT THE AUTHOR

USA Today bestselling author, Elise Faber, loves chocolate, Star Wars, Harry Potter, and hockey (the order depending on the day and how well her team -- the Sharks! -- are playing). She and her husband also play as much hockey as they can squeeze into their schedules, so much so that their typical date night is spent on the ice. Elise is the mom to two exuberant boys and lives in Northern California. Connect with her in her Facebook group, the Fabinators or find more information about her books at www.elisefaber.com.

facebook.com/elisefaberauthor

amazon.com/author/elisefaber

bookbub.com/profile/elise-faber

instagram.com/elisefaber

goodreads.com/elisefaber

pinterest.com/elisefaberwrite